Hank Vogel

La femme nue

Editions le Stylophile

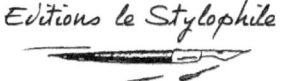

La femme nue

Essai très déshabillé, décent et non provocateur écrit dans un style, mon préféré, que
j'ai baptisé sous le regard de Dieu de *répé-
titif mais plus proche du langage des
anges*.

1

Je cherche la femme nue. Nue de la tête aux pieds. Nue corps et âme. Nue du premier janvier au trente-et-un décembre. Nue pour être aimée pour sa nudité toute nue. Cette dernière phrase m'étonne. La nudité m'étonne aussi. Seule la vraie nudité n'étonne personne. Pour moi, le mot nudité est synonymie de perfection. Je recommence. Je cherche la femme parfaite. Physiquement parfaite. Mentalement parfaite. Moralement parfaite. Amoureusement parfaite. Librement parfaite. Parfaitement parfaite. Mais cette perfection que je cherche est-elle vraiment parfaite? Je recommence de nouveau. Non, je commence à me faire une idée. Bien que c'est difficile. Car la femme est un monstre sacré d'élégance, d'érotisme et de talentueux sentiments. Tant pis pour moi, j'ai décidé de découvrir la femme nue, j'irai donc jusqu'au bout de cette décision. Suis-je en train de m'égarer? La femme m'a toujours fait perdre la tête. À tous les hommes, d'ailleurs. À presque tous les hommes. Même aux femmes elles-mêmes. Quelle folie! Quelle étrange tentative!

2

Un corps nu, de femme, me fait des appels... Son oeil est plus grand que son ventre. Son ventre plus gros que ses cuisses. Ses cuisses plus grosses que ses fesses. Et ses fesses plus intelligentes que sa cervelle. Quel étrange animal! Je fuis. J'ai peur. Mon éducation me dit que la femme n'est pas une automobile, ni un bateau, ni un train, ni une gare, ni un port, ni une porcherie. Alors quel est ce corps nu qui me fait des appels de *farde*? C'est le corps d'une femme qui vous allume pour vous éteindre, qui vous expose ses charmes trop charnels pour mourir à sa solitude, qui vous attire vers elle pour ressusciter de sa médiocrité. C'est en observant ce genre de femme que mon imagination s'approche de l'imagination démesurée d'un auteur de films d'horreur. Je hais ce genre de femme parce qu'il fait du tort à la femme.

3

Elle a souvent le ventre rond. Sa chevelure est douce. Son sourire est pour sourire. Et ses cris sont ceux de la prudence. Ses mains ne cessent de caresser, de laver et de repasser. Son coeur est une citadelle de tranquillité. Pour le héros comme pour le traître. Son corps est une nudité de tendresse. Mal habillé ou bien vêtu, il est éternellement transparent. Et son sexe est inexistant. Elle a le coeur sur la main et la vie dans le ventre. Elle porte malheureusement le surnom le plus exploité de tous les temps, le nom délicieux de maman.

4

Pour le citadin, la mise à nu féminine n'est qu'un déshabillage provocateur. Quelle triste réalité! Le citadin porte les jours sans soleil des lunettes noires pour découvrir cette nudité légère et superficielle tout en protégeant sa nudité obsessionnelle.

5

Un con nu à moins de deux mètres de mes yeux a déclaré la guerre à mes sens. Je perds le nord. Je perds le sud. L'est et l'ouest sont trop politisés. Je me laisse aller tantôt vert le haut, tantôt vers le bas. Plus facilement vers le bas. Ou vers les bas. Si seulement ils étaient noirs! Ils sont gris. Gris comme ces maisons grises peintes de toutes les couleurs. Gris comme la mort. Gris comme ces oiseaux gris qui sifflent le malheur du monde. Les bas ont disparu. Les jambes qui les portaient également. Je n'ai pas eu le temps de rêver. Les tables qui sont autour de moi sont vides. Les chaises respirent de légèreté. Les grosses fesses sont allées écraser d'autres tissus. La femme est absente. La femme nue invisible. La fumée des cigarettes essaye de la remplacer. La machine de l'imaginaire fait marche arrière. Je me jette dans les bras de mon enfance. Une fée aux yeux brillants de douceur me berce et m'allaite de ses

agréables seins qui sentent bon la tendresse. J'avale ma dernière goutte de café et
m'en vais vivre ailleurs.

6

Je vous il, nous vous ils. Jeux, vous, île. J'ai des articles à vendre. Des articles d'article. Des jeux de mots. Et des mots vides. Je vous ailes, nous vous ailes. J'ai des mots légers à vendre. Des mots qui planent dans les airs. Des mots nus pour habiller une femme trop nue. Une femme qui aurait perdu sa fraîcheur et le don de s'habiller. J'ai tout ce qu'il faut pour éclairer les coins les plus sombres de votre première mémoire, mesdames, mesdemoiselles, vierges et déesses!

7

Or est sa chevelure. Dorées sont mes intentions. Ses yeux noisette me rappellent les
printemps de ma jeunesse où je confondais
les femmes avec les ombres des arbres.
Blanche est sa peau. Blanche comme un
nuage à peine rose. Sa nudité me ferait
voyager à travers des paysages de soie et de
coton. Que les anges de la sagesse viennent
à mon secours!

8

Des mains soignées. Les doigts longs. Les ongles limés et vernis. Une bague presque à chaque doigt. Elles tournent les pages du journal du matin. Le papier tremble d'émotion. Je sens vibrer l'ex tronc d'arbre...

9

Pages, cages, sages. L'un vient, l'autre suit. La rivière de nos intelligences momentanées suit son mouvement. Elle se jette dans le fleuve des relations humaines. Elle devient amour quand elle entre dans l'océan des lumières inexpliquées. La femme nue se baigne dans ces eaux limpides et calmes. Son savoir est un jeu de regards, un jeu innocent. Elle est là page après page, ligne a près ligne, mot après mot. Elle sourit maternellement à chacune de mes maladresses. Elle purifie le bleu de mes yeux quand la monotonie jaillit du fond de mon âme. Elle refroidit le sang bouillant de ma colère. Elle me libère de mes cages, de ces faux abris que j'ai construits pour me protéger des éventuels vents chargés d'illusion. La femme nue marche dans le désert. Avec élégance. Sans crainte, sans douleur. Elle marche vers l'infini. Le poète la suit traînant derrière lui ses nombreuses montagnes de mots incorrectes. Il la suit attiré par sa nudité, cette nudité qui dégage un puissant parfum de noblesse: la noblesse de l'âme.

10

Quand elle était nue, elle semblait tout habillée et quand elle était habillée, elle semblait toute nue. Sans doute, aurait-elle dû choisir un autre couturier? Un couturier moins tiré à quatre épingles. Un couturier japonais attaché aux vieilles traditions de l'empire du soleil levant. Ainsi le jour, on aurait pu lire sur son visage la nudité de ses sentiments et le soir, au lit, on aurait pu découvrir la vraie nudité de son corps. Certaines éducations orientales ont des effets secondaires primordiaux pour la sauvegarde de l'espèce humaine.

11

Dans une région sauvage, une jeune fille sauvage se moquait des hommes trop sauvages. Elle se moquait à sa façon, en camouflant sa nudité, sa nudité sauvage. Souvent les hommes devenaient fous. Fous de ce camouflage. Selon eux, cette chose étrange mettait trop en évidence la nudité de la jeune fille. Ils devenaient fous surtout quand leur rêve ne devenait réalité. Et inversement. Un jour, lasse de se donner en spectacle, elle épousa un jeune homme de passage qui refusait de se montrer nu. Ensemble, ils découvrirent la richesse de leur nudité secrète.

12

Je suis quelque part en montagne. La neige n'est, cette année-là, qu'une légère couverture de soie de Chine. Les skieurs marchent comme des prisonniers, un boulet à chaque pied, une chaussure à chaque jambe. Ils marchent en direction d'un lieu paradisiaque. Ils font des efforts surhumains pour ensuite glisser comme des dieux descendant tout droit des nuages. Moi, je regarde, j'observe, je surmonte les obstacles des plaisirs hivernaux. Une bonne femme de neige m'attend près d'une colonie de jeunes sapins. Mirage ou désir profond? Je crois que je vais me transformer en stalactite de glace pour percer le mystère de cette nudité quasi polaire.

13

J'aime les cailles
Et les poissons sans écailles
J'aime les feux de paille
Et les femmes de grande taille
J'aime les maillots à grosses mailles
Et les amours sans faille
J'aime où que j'aille
Voir s'éloigner les canailles
Car j'aime est le contraire de aïe!

Chère Vous,

 Ce petit poème vous est destiné. Je l'ai écrit pour vous faire oublier le vide creusé par vos éternelles questions. Ces questions sans réponse. Car trop habillé, le coeur bat en retraite. Libre comme l'air, il se tait et absorbe les liqueurs de l'existence. Digérez mon poème, il est moins nocif qu'une bouffée d'opium. Digérez-le ou avalez-le tout cru pour l'amour des mots. Je sais, vous avez soif de bonheur. Moi, j'ai soif de sourires, de vous voir sourire.

14

14 février 1989. Vive la Saint-Valentin! La nudité est à la fête. Celle du corps et de l'esprit. Quand tout va bien, bien entendu. Quand Roméo et Juliette sont sur le même balcon. Quand les parents et les ennemis de l'amour sont à cent mille lieux du jardin d'Éden. Quand le serpent a mangé sa queue. Quand la pomme est sans pépins.

15

J'ai valsé toute la nuit avec les ombres de l'au-delà. À cheval entre la mort et la vie éternelle, elles m'ont fait savoir que pour entrer dans le coeur des voies célestes, il fallait que je dénude ma nudité, que je lui enlève les pardessus étouffants de mon imagination. Je n'ai pas osé obéir, j'ai pensé à un coup monté de la déesse de l'imaginaire.

16

17 février 1989. Ce matin, j'ai entendu siffler, chanter les oiseaux. Je bloque ma boîte à message, le printemps n'est pas à négliger en cette saison. Je me tais donc et me laisse vivre.

17

Quand la publicité dégage une forte odeur de ridicule, je me sens nu, sans la moindre richesse, sans le moindre désir dans ma peau, mais libre comme le vent. Souvent la publicité pue l'exagération, le mensonge et l'adoration du dieu argent. Pour moi, le meilleur, le merveilleux et le divin s'approchent du silence.

18

Trop parler plonge l'orateur dans un profond vide. Un vide sans espace, plein d'ombre, l'ombre des mots.

19

Je n'ai toujours pas découvert le vent de la béatitude, ce vent capable d'effacer à jamais les incompréhensibles maladresses dessinées sur le vaste désert de ma mémoire. Faut-il que je me dise: bien vieillir, c'est mourir au présent et rajeunir, c'est mourir au passé?

20

Son visage n'avait pas avancé d'une semelle sur la marche du temps mais son derrière avait doublé de volume. Il (d'elle) s'était, sans doute, trop vite pressé de s'installer dans le fauteuil du salon de ses rêves. J'ai baisé la nudité de sa peau maternelle. Là où les larmes arrivent au galop pour se jeter sans retenue dans le vide.

21

Entre la fille peintre qui peint avec ses problèmes et la dactylo qui compose avec nonchalance, je choisirai la première qui me fera don de sa nudité, de sa totale nudité. En récompense, je lui dévoilerai tous mes secrets. Ceux de mes mots et ceux de mes maux. La poésie fonctionnera comme juge.

22

24 février 1989. Six heures trente-cinq du matin. La neige tombe à gros flocons. Elle a décidé de vêtir la terre pour une belle cérémonie. La mère de nos éternelles racines a trop souffert de sa nudité, de cette nudité provoquée par la main dévastatrice de l'homme. Vais-je mettre des gants et garder ma tête froide dans un chapeau de timidité? J'espère que non. Avec la neige, l'horizon est presque inexistant. Avec un peu de chance, mes nobles pensées feront boule de neige. Je suis si prudent que je marche sur la pointe des pieds. Pour éviter la noyade. Car je rêve de baignades chaudes et parfumées de douceur aux anti-podes des feux de l'enfer.

23

L'artiste contemple l'océan.
Le critique, lui, ouvre tout grand ses yeux
mais ne voit qu'un lac.

24

Dehors: la pluie et le vent. Dedans: ton corps et mon corps. Deux corps ne faisant plus qu'un. Un corps illuminé par une lune de miel souriante et rêveuse. Seul le drap noir du présent sera témoin de nos caresses. Je mordrai légèrement tes doigts longs aux ongles arrachés par ta nervosité pour te faire savoir que j'accepte tout de toi. Je mordrai avec délicatesse le bout de tes lèvres pour mieux goûter la saveur de celles-ci. Je baiserai tes pieds pour t'annoncer que je suis ton fidèle serviteur. Que la pluie m'écoute et que le vent emporte vers toi mes désirs.

25

Loin de toute cathédrale, je chanterai silencieusement *dans* tes oreilles les airs harmonieux de l'au-delà. Ils t'apporteront la paix et l'enthousiasme. Un enthousiasme qui te permettra d'organiser ta vie avec souplesse et dignité. La fontaine de mes mots te fera oublier le temps de nos séparations. Des séparations momentanées dues aux prisons de mon devoir. Il exige de moi beaucoup de sacrifice. Il exige de toi beaucoup de patience. Le monde te fera des misères et je m'occuperai de la misère du monde. Nous surmonterons les obstacles des imprévus avec allégresse. Grâce à toi, je renaîtrai au pouvoir de l'art. Et j'aurai une place dans le jardin où la rose éternelle remet tout en question. Nous serons toujours nus face à nos secrets et tout mal habillés face aux mensonges. Je n'exige rien de toi. Je ne veux que t'aimer.

26

Tel un oiseau sur un fil électrique, je suis sur le fil du désir. Cet habitat, qui n'est à l'abri d'aucune violence, n'est que provisoire. Vais-je me lancer dans le vide pour découvrir enfin la nudité espérée? Le courage ne me manque pas. Ce sont le spectre de l'échec et l'ombre de la mort qui noircissent mon ciel. Seconde après seconde, je supplie les anges de la réussite de venir à mon secours.

27

Comme le peintre attaché à certaines couleurs, le poète est attaché à certains mots.

L'un et l'autre se répètent en étalant sur le champ blanc de la création les fantômes de leurs attachements.

28

Les pensées vont et viennent. Les nuages vont et viennent. Les amours vont et viennent. Seul l'arbre qui est solide comme un roc ne perd que ses feuilles dans la tempête. Nu et blessé, il permet à la terre de se nourrir. L'homme, lui, nu et blessé, ne nourrit plus personne.

29

Si elle est chatte et moi chien, si elle est de glace et moi de feu, si elle respire l'air de l'ouest et moi l'air de l'est, toute marche vers le meilleur finira par un recul.

30

Ouvre-moi le portail de ton royaume, déesse de mes espérances! J'ai hâte de me blottir contre toi. L'odeur et la chaleur de ton corps si divin m'allaiteront pour la vie et je mourrai au désespoir. Pour l'instant, je n'ai aperçu qu'une lucarne, une si lointaine lucarne.

31

Il est temps que je cesse de réclamer justice. Si je suis, *et surtout ai été*, bon avec les sables, le désert arrêtera la tempête et je découvrirai l'oasis.

32

Quand le désir est là, le plaisir est dans les airs.

Quand le plaisir est là, le désir est dans les cendres.

33

Quand le désir forge ma mémoire, le puits du passé se transforme en un étrange monument tout biscornu autour duquel l'ignorance et la peur se courent après.

34

Sous la pluie, les rues sont des miroirs gris
où la folie citadine a de la peine à refléter.

35

Si l'homme n'avait que le langage verbal pour s'exprimer et communiquer, l'accouplement se ferait dans un discours d'injures, d'insultes et de promesses trompeuses.

36

Seul, je suis le roi.
Accompagné, je suis déjà un serviteur.

37

Il a fallu qu'une femme me fît perdre la tête pour que je retrouve ma vieille tête silencieuse qui ignore tout des jeux de l'amour. Le merle est redevenu singe. Et la branche arbre.

38

C'est dans les difficultés que l'on reconnaît ses amis.

C'est dans l'obscurité que l'on reconnaît un vrai amour.

39

Il voulait être nu, il s'est retrouvé tout habillé. Il voulait découvrir la femme nue, il a rencontré des femmes voilées qui cherchaient l'homme nu. Déçu de son échec, il se mit à inventer des mots, des phrases puis des récits. Mais la femme nue était toujours invisible. Déçu une seconde fois, il força le jeux et se retrouva tout nu dans un lit d'hôpital. Et un soir, la mort, qui passait par là, lui dit:

- Comme il est triste de constater que l'homme attende la dernière heure pour se décider à comprendre que la nudité n'est autre chose que le parfum de la vie. Tu avais soif de nudité et tu t'es gavé de voiles. Tu t'es mis au lit quand tu aurais dû te mettre à table. Ta as ouvert ta bouche quand tu aurais dû ouvrir tes yeux.

40

Celui qui ne lutte que pour atteindre le sanctuaire, n'atteindra que le vestibule. Car le saint des saints est le coeur de la sagesse, du non-agir.

41

L'amour peut être extrême.
La nudité ne peut être que totale.

42

Depuis quelques temps, trop d'âmes para-
lysées rodent autour de moi. Elles me
sucent le sang. Si je leur faisais confiance,
elles seraient capables de me faire croire
que la nudité est dans le squelette. Le sucre
est amère. Le sel doux. Les jardins sont
dévastés par la colère de l'ignorance. Les
voiles déchirés. Les masques arrachés.
Résultat: le vide est là. Mon erreur: c'est
ma démarche. La femme nue est dans les
airs et non pas dans les cendres. Peut-être
au-delà des airs. Mais en tout cas pas dans
les cendres. La femme nue est éternelle.
Son parfum n'a ni jeunesse ni vieillesse.
Un parfum qui chasse les fortes odeurs du
passé avec une force angélique. Un parfum
qui sent bon la mère. la soeur l'épouse, la
fille, la maîtresse, la complice d'un sourire...

43

3 mars 1989. Sept heures du matin. Je me rends compte que face à la nudité, je ne suis qu'un analphabète, un analphabète trop chiquement habillé.

Être et avoir

1

Le mot est sacré. Mais faut-il que ce soit un sacré mot! Je suis prêt. Je suis libre. J'ai décidé de conquérir le monde des mots. Avec mes mots et mes maux. À la conquête de la chimie du verbe. Au creux de la vague de mes idées. L'erreur m'accompagne. Le courage est collé à ma chair. Les oiseaux de ma jeunesse ont abandonné le nid de mes sentiments. Ces message(r)s que j'adorais sont maintenant auprès du Père céleste. Suis-je en train d'exagérer? Probablement. Pas forcément. Suis-je un écrivain honnête? La gloire ou l'anonymat seront mes juges. Un jour. À l'aube des temps nouveaux. Quand les papillons ne feront plus peur aux fleurs du printemps. J'aime être ivre de mes phrases absurdes. Elles me propulsent dans une étrange béatitude. C'est là que je me sens riche. Vraiment riche.

2

De désespoir, le singe se gratte comme un fou.

De désespoir, le poète gratte le papier comme un fou.

L'un est amoureux d'une guenon qui est indifférente à ses singeries.

L'autre est amoureux d'une jeune femme qui est indifférente à ses poésies.

De désespoir, le singe et l'homme se sont réunis et ont signé un pacte d'alliance afin de fortifier leur espoir.

3
La femme, cet homme si séduisant!

4

Le poète est un être vulnérable qui porte en lui, sans trop se plaindre de son sort, les blessures du monde.

5

Une pluie de mots est tombée cette nuit.

Une pluie de larmes est tombée ce matin.

Une pluie de sable tombera prochaine-
ment.

Loin des orages, je suis poète.

En pleine pluie, je suis mouillé de la tête
aux pieds, ni plus ni moins.

6

Dans l'être, il y a l'avoir.

Dans l'avoir, il n'y a que l'avoir, un avoir désireux de ne jamais être.

7

Le monde des mots n'est pas un monde sans maux. Mais en posant des mots, certains maux disparaissent.

8

Répétition: le passé revient à la charge. C'est l'impossibilité de mourir aux vieilles idées.

9

Mort, le poète est vivant dans le coeur des hommes.

Vivant, il est mourant dans leur esprit.

10

Quand la raison est au coin de la rue, l'asphalte est un ciel immaculé.

Quand la folie est au bout du chemin, le sol est inexistant.

11

La prière est dans l'avoir,
Le pardon dans l'être.
Le désir est dans l'avoir,
Le plaisir dans l'être.
La complexité est dans l'avoir,
La simplicité dans l'être.
La haine est dans l'avoir,
L'amour dans l'être.
La guerre est dans l'avoir,
La paix dans l'être.
L'avoir est ailleurs.
L'être est ici.
L'avoir ne mène à rien.
L'être mène à tout.

12

Ah, ces odeurs qui nous chatouillent l'esprit!

Ah, ces parfums qui nous tourmentent l'âme!

Je cours de-ci delà à la recherche d'un brin de bonheur.

Dans ma poche droite, je n'ai que des reproches.

Dans la gauche, j'ai les sourires et les caresses de mes proches.

Je n'ai plus de chapeau pour saluer bien bas les professeurs de ma matière grise.

J'ai la tête haute et le regard lointain.

La philosophie du simple est sans doute la seule qui *soit* dans le vrai.

Nous sommes le 10 mars 1989. C'est mon anniversaire. Dieu m'a déjà fait son cadeau. Aux premières couleurs bleues du jour. Je n'avais ni âge ni raison, j'étais bien dans ma peau.

13

La poésie me permet d'être. Elle m'encourage à ne plus avoir. Les images vont et viennent mais ne s'installent jamais. Ni aux cimes de mes espoirs, ni aux creux de mes désespoirs. Je ne suis qu'un spectateur. Un spectateur qui tousse à chaque caprice du mal. Un spectateur qui sourit à chaque caresse du bien. Je suis dans les nuages. Souvent. Tel un oiseau. Tel un papillon. Tel un ange. Mon voyage est fabuleux. Le spectacle est grandiose. Grandiose est trop faible ou trop lourd pour définir l'indéfinissable. La femme est absente quand je voyage. Seul l'homme est présent. Un homme sans sexe mais muni d'une cervelle magique. Quand la poésie m'enveloppe, je ne suis plus poète, je suis la poésie.

14

Quand la femme marche, l'homme traîne.
Quand la femme traîne, l'homme marche à
fond.

15

Trois pommes, deux poires et un brin d'attention, je me sens le maître de l'univers. La nuit est blanche. Le ciel est de velours. La lune est brillante et souriante. Les étoiles délicatement pointent la voûte céleste. L'avoir sommeille tout au fond de ma poche. L'être est total. La femme aimée, nue sous un voile transparent, m'invite à son festin de mots doux et de caresses sublimes. Refuser serait un crime contre l'humanité. Je n'ai rien à perdre, au contraire, j'ai tout à être.

16

L'eau purifie le sang.
Le vin purifie le chagrin.
L'amour purifie l'âme.

17

Le végétal engendre le végétal.
L'animal engendre l'animal.
L'homme engendre l'homme.
La haine engendre la haine.
L'amour engendre l'amour.
Seul le silence engendre le merveilleux.

18

Allongé sous un hêtre, je n'ai rien.
Allongé sous un hêtre, je suis tout.

19

J'habite une maison qui n'est pas à moi.

Je roule dans une voiture qui n'est pas à moi.

Je travaille dans une usine qui n'est pas à moi.

Je dors avec une femme qui n'est pas à moi mais à elle-même.

Je suis le père de deux enfants qui ne sont à moi mais à eux-mêmes.

J'ai un passeport qui n'est pas à moi mais à mon pays.

Je vis dans un pays qui n'est pas à moi mais aux autres.

J'ai chez moi un tas de choses qui ne sont pas à moi mais aux miens qui ne sont pas à moi mais à eux-même.

Tout ce que j'ai de vraiment à moi, c'est la certitude que rien n'est à moi.

Même les mots, qui proviennent de moi, une fois sur le papier, ne sont plus à moi. Et en réfléchissant bien, ils n'ont jamais été a moi, ils étaient aux autres.

Alors, que les autres fassent autant avec moi!

20

Havane, loukoum et café turc. Du soleil à gogo. Un petit nuage de passage et voilà que je pars à la découverte d'une société nouvelle, d'une citadelle, d'un château, d'un puits, d'une ruine, d'un cimetière, d'un balcon, d'une Juliette sans Roméo, d'une fée, d'un sage, d'un prophète, d'un dieu miséricordieux et Dieu sait qui ou quoi encore. J'ai tout pour réussir sauf la réussite.

Havane, loukoum et café turc, le verbe avoir perd pied, le verbe être gagne des ailes tout en risquant de perdre quelques plumes.

21

Quand le soleil est au zénith, je me sens explorateur.

Quand le soleil se couche, je me sens poète.

Quand le soleil se lève, je suis un travailleur qui commence à sentir la douleur du travail (désorganisé).

Grâce au soleil, j'ai la notion du temps, de ce temps qui file, file sans le moindre désir de s'arrêter.

22

Quand les anges se déguisent en démons, l'amour s'alourdit.

Quand les anges se métamorphosent en démons, l'amour devient haine.

Quand les anges perdent espoir, l'amour s'envole.

Quand les anges planent, l'amour commence à s'installer.

Quand les anges sont installés, l'amour est là.

23

Ne dites jamais à un prophète que vous manquez d'eau!

Ne dites jamais à un poète que vous manquez de parfum!

Car l'un et l'autre seraient capables de faire basculer le système solaire pour vous prouver le contraire.

24

J'ai le cœur fatigué, l'esprit usé, la mémoire surchargée... J'ai combattu pour un roi imaginaire. J'ai cherché en vain la reine de mes rêves. Je suis las de tous ces combats où la victoire méprise la joie, où le plaisir s'envole à la fin de l'effort.

Je fus empereur, esclave, ange, renard, eau, feu, sagesse, colère, prince, maudit, adoré le temps d'un sourire. Le temps d'un échange de mots. Le temps d'une illusion. Mathématiquement, je suis loin d'être une droite ou une courbe. Encore moins une parabole ou une hyperbole. Je m'approche de la sinusoïde. De cette parfaite imparfaite sinusoïde. J'ai eu trop soif, trop faim, trop envie d'être pris pour ce ou celui que je n'étais pas. Qui suis-je? Que suis-je? Une éléphant rose? Une souris verte? À cheval entre la chenille et le papillon? En pleine erreur? Ruiné, je ramasse encore les miettes de mes incroyables festins. Vais-je comprendre un jour que la poursuite du vent est une lutte insensée et que le désir d'être et la sensation d'être trahissent la réalité, trahissent l'être.

25

Je n'ai qu'un seul ennemi, l'ombre de ma colère.

En colère, je suis en pleine guerre, je suis déjà un assassin.

26

Rupture! Je me suis libéré de ces chaînes qui me liaient à des passions devenues trop quotidiennes.

27

La misère est un mal impardonnable lorsqu'elle est provoquée par un autre mal encore plus impardonnable: l'insouciance.

28

Nu et hésitant, face à une femme, j'ai l'allure d'un singe et la mémoire d'un éléphant.

Nu et sans mémoire, face à une femme, je suis face à moi-même. Les formes sont volupté. Et les couleurs douceur.

29

J'ai entre les doigts l'outil qui aiguise mon pouvoir. Pour rien au monde, je l'échangerais.

Exceptionnellement, je l'échangerais, non sans regret, contre une vie éternelle. Mais une vie éternelle sans pouvoir ni savoir.

30

Enfant, j'étais le roi du monde.

Jeune homme, j'étais le roi de mes conquêtes.

Vieillard, je ne serai plus que le roi de mes souvenirs.

31

Dans la jungle, le lion est le maître de la force, le singe le maître du rire.

Dans notre société, certains politiciens sont des lions qui font sourire, rire et pleurer.

Dans la jungle, c'est la jungle.

Dans notre société, c'est la jungle qui subit les assauts de la civilisation.

32

Le mensonge est bavardage, la vérité silence.

Le mensonge brûle les étapes, la vérité éteint les tempêtes.

33

La vérité chagrine les menteurs lorsqu'elle dévoile le mensonge.

C'est le seul mal qu'elle peut faire indépendamment de sa volonté.

34

J'ai dormi dans les bras d'un sommeil qui avait les bras longs.

Avec un rien, il me faisait un tout. Et tout n'avait rien de compliqué.

Le coeur était sur chaque main. Et les mains se tenaient par la main.

J'étais si bien dans les bras de ce sommeil qu'il m'a fallu plusieurs heures avant que je me décide à me réveiller.

Sans doute, avait-il des bras trop longs pour mes idées si courtes et mes intentions si lentes?

35

Trop sûre et fière de sa beauté, elle finira dans le piège de la laideur.

Au-delà du beau er du laid, du bien et du mal, une larme vaut un sourire et le blas-phème vaut la prière

36

Le poète n'est pas le maître de ses poèmes,
il n'est que l'esclave de sa poésie. Mais un
esclave consentant.

37

J'ai chassé de ma cage aux oiseaux l'aigle impérial, le faucon égyptien et la chouette de mes escapades nocturnes.

J'ai agrandi la cage jusqu'aux frontières de mes paisibles espérances.

Puis, j'ai ouvert les portes et la cage est devenue un refuge pour mes oiseaux timides.

Et maintenant, l'harmonie n'est plus ailleurs. Le vent est modeste et les orages sont mineurs et appréciés.

38

La vanité d'être est une affaire d'avoir.

Ne plus espérer d'être nous plonge dans l'être.

39

L'avoir est une citadelle qui tombe en ruine.

L'être est une forteresse sans muraille ni portail.

40

Je suis me permet de le rester.
J'ai m'empêche d'être.

J'ai donne faim.
Je suis met fin à toute faim.

Quand j'ai, je ne suis plus.
Quand je suis, j'ignore l'avoir.

L'avoir est limité.
L'être, infini.

L'un est amour-propre.
L'autre, amour.

SNUFF

By Eric Enck and Adam Huber

I0682985

Snuff Books
Philadelphia, PA
snuffbooks.com

Artwork by Stella Price
Snuff Books Logo, and associated logos are trademarks and/or
registered trademarks of Snuff Books.

ISBN: 0-9818967-2-3
ISBN 13: 978-0-9818967-2-4

Printed in the U.S.A.

Second Edition 2009

This book is dedicated to my family, friends, and enemies

-Eric Enck

For Chris. You've been like a brother to me and never ceased encouraging my ridiculous whims.

-Adam Huber

Prologue

Jack Sanders drove down the serpentine road that led out of town and into the hills as if he were being pursued by a horde of demon women. Without thinking, he took the same route he'd taken with Amanda several times up to Mallow Drive, ages ago, long before he cut her eyes out.

Jack opened the window of the car as he drove, welcoming a sobering breeze against his face. But it had very little effect. There was too much alcohol in his blood and too much panic to make him much of a driver on such a notoriously tricky stretch of road. He didn't care. He just wanted to put some distance between himself and that world as fast as possible.

On one of the hairpin bends, his clammy hands slid on the wheel, and he momentarily lost control of the car. He was a good enough driver—even in his present state—to recover quickly, and things might have been fine had another speed freak not come barreling around the corner. His drink-slurred foot was too slow on the brake to stop the car from sliding. There was no barrier between him and the embankment. Jack's GTO hit the tree with a smash of glass that rang out in one voice, and then…that was all.

* * *

In moments, he awoke. The daze of blood blurring Jack's eyes was quickly gone, and he wiped his hand across his face and saw in the distance a flipped over Mercedes S-Class.

He decided on impulse.

Perhaps his day wouldn't be over after all. Jack kicked open the side window of his car and exited the wreck with his broken and bruised face in shambles. He saw the cunt that had passed him—wearing a middle finger and a smile—now lying in a daze. She was maybe seventeen, her daddy's car no doubt. Jack stood in shock, his determined mind spinning out of control from the Patron, as smooth as a young girl's vulva.

Jack had a grim view. He estimated inner life was no more than a vaguely self-aware mirror. It was the perfect line of defense to have in a decade where deconstruction and simulacra were prime subjects in every pedant's droning mantra.

He was invigorated from escaping death.

The argument was made then—as a means of defending the idea to not save the young girl—and it was admirable he nearly had himself convinced. It was an art that Jack would insist get inside situations and personalities rather than hover in godly fashion over the mess. It was the difference between being in a traffic helicopter over the freeway and actually being behind the wheel, in the midst of it all. In the midst of wanting to rape a defenseless girl.

The problem with making the case for an actor like Jack, who had been on the outs with mainstream cinema, was that the plausible case got passed up altogether and overstatement became the rule. Ego was one of Jack's flaws, the mistake that accumulation equals worth, value and importance. Sometimes it worked, yet even actors who have performed in brilliant films will produce a long and profoundly under-edited dud. Many actors, even washed-up ones like Jack Sanders, would have benefited greatly from the advice of the crusading monks at the City of Beziers.

Kill them all; God will know his own...

The only problem was there's no money to be made in such sweeping strategies.

* * *

Jack had always struck critics as someone who would be a perfectly competent criminal, one step away from a serial killer and two steps towards a drug dealer—an edgy combination of Albert Fish and Patrick Bateman—if he weren't so busy gussying up his sensationalist subjects with the window dressing of eviscerated narcissism.

But there are limits to how long a moviegoer can gaze into an abyss, or listen to the limitless chatter of character minds that have lost a soul-giving personality. Crime fiction, a form predicated on supreme measures of reserve and clinical flatness, might have been an ideal medium for the rigor-mortised humanity Jack loved to describe. The procedural aspects would have imposed some properly ascribed limits on his story lines and enabled him to create with greater aim.

Jack Sanders knew he was exactly right on this point as he pulled the young blonde from the car and yanked both her broken arms loosely behind her back. He felt the fragments beneath her flesh move ever so nimbly as he ripped her schoolyard skirt free, and his hard cock thrust into her barely stretched vagina. He knew for a fact she was seventeen.

As he fulfilled his contract with the young blonde—who he knew had a name between Amy and Stacey—raping her and laughing at her screams, drilling her from behind with such style and grace, the measures of horrific timing and the required component for wit to sting deeper was absent from that screen and in even sparser supply with blood and flesh.

The crime genre would have liberated Jack from struggling to act through his themes under the crushing burden of art.

Even as he stabbed the cheerleader in the back several times, still fucking her on the hood of her car as she lay dying in a sea of blood and brake fluid, the difference remained. These actors were artists, describing a skilled application of craft.

Jack's vice conveyed pose, pose, pose…

Drama is the word.

Not help me.

I've heard that enough. This bitch here has screamed it for the last ten minutes.

* * *

Jack placed his hands against the half flipped over car—the moonlight always made blood look different—and he came down her ass, in her secret chambers, that like her, had nothing more to say. He spent the time contemplating writing his name in blood and semen all over daddy's favorite little girl.

* * *

"I hate fucking critics," Jack barked at the moon. He was breathing heavy, thinking of his last curtain call. A washed-up, rarely working actor, Jack needed to get back into the business as soon as possible.

Part I:
Entrepreneurial Spirit

Chapter One

We're all critics. Most of us just don't do it for a living.

Despite the clichés of the "open minded" and the ultimate decisions you think are best left up to whatever your skewed version of a personal god is: we're all guilty. Go ahead, walk down the street, go shopping, and mind your business, we're watching. We're judging.

The old man with a weathered heart full of staunch racism, he's watching you. The gossipy, middle-aged Christian education director; loitering rich kids dressed in chic, pre-torn jeans; soccer moms with fading looks and cesarean section scars; pot-bellied NASCAR fans and all the other less-than-perfect but better-than-you bystanders, they've all got their eyes on you.

* * *

Jack was well aware of the scrutiny ahead as he used a bottom incisor to scrape Amy's blood from beneath his manicured fingernails. The next-morning cleanup was almost worse than the hangover.

Almost, Jack thought, as he threw up bile and the bits of dried blood into the sink...*At least I can skip the gym today.*

Wiping his mouth, tasting a hint of iron and pussy mixed with the anti-bacterial soap on his hands, Jack grabbed a glass of whiskey—long ago watered down by melted ice—off the back of the toilet and used it to wash down a handful of store-brand pain relievers. The whiskey stung the cuts on his bottom lip, and he wretched a little as the intercom to his apartment buzzed from the other room.

Pulling on stained boxer shorts, he walked through the sparsely decorated living room and over to the stereo, turning on the remastered version of a Bob Geldof record and pushing the volume up loud enough to cover the stifled cries coming from inside the spare bedroom. Jack signed for the package and closed the door without a word, feeling the deliveryman staring past him at the empty bottles and mold-blackened Chinese takeout containers piling up in the kitchen.

God bless expedited shipping. Jack smiled as he picked at the tape holding the box closed. *You never know when you're going to have a surprise project.*

Mail order, #11 surgical blades, cleanliness in your finger tips and just in time.

Just next to godliness after all.

Last night had turned out to be more than just a few minutes of fun. As Jack had wiped down the accident scene, scouring away his own blood and come dripping from the girl's ass and dousing the scene in ammonia, he noticed the two of them weren't alone. Slumped over in the passenger's seat was another girl, maybe a year older than Amy.

* * *

When I woke up everything seemed muffled. Light cracked in from behind whatever was wrapped around my eyes, but I couldn't make anything out.

The last thing I remembered was seeing him grinning, pulling his cock—glistening with blood—back into his jeans. The last thing I remembered before waking up here was a rag being shoved into my mouth, the taste of ammonia making my eyes water. Numbness and the faint sting of broken glass, that's all I remembered.

There were noises coming from the other room and the flicker of TV images played behind my eyes.

Most of the feeling was gone from my body, and something was cutting into my wrists, which were tied behind my back. It was cold, and the rag was still in my mouth.

There was blood everywhere.

Why was there so much blood?

What the fuck was playing on the TV?

Why is this all past tense?

* * *

With the sun now coming in through the picture windows of the living room, Jack squinted, trying to delay the onset of the day ahead. Another day of waiting. Another bit part and condescending casting directors, but surgical equipment and top shelf liquor weren't free. Keeping up an image cost money.

There are still a few hours before the grind, still time to take one step closer.

The cries from the other room had died down. "I Don't Like Mondays" would have to wait. She would be saved, freed from the ingrained images and societal expectations. Saved from her parents' doting and hopes. In a few more hours, they would never have to worry again.

Jack could hear rumblings from whatever Italian exploitation flick was on loop on the TV as he cracked the door. She was on her side, arms handcuffed behind her back, a sliver of her twat poking out from the side of her panties. He'd had to cut off her designer jeans last night because they were snagged on a shard of steel from the door. It just made it easier today.

She half grunted as he lifted her up, fingering the metal blade and pulling the makeshift blindfold up from her left eye. The razor edge of it was halfway behind her eye before she screamed and the blade hit the optic nerve. One down. By the time her second eye was out, Jack's hard-on was back.

After removing what remained of her tattered clothes, Jack flipped the TV over to a cable cooking show before tracing the blade down the small of her back—her ID said her name was Samantha, 19 years old. By now she could barely groan, and when the blade cut slowly across her asshole nothing registered. Just to be safe, Jack had crushed her windpipe, making sure the neighbors couldn't hear. Making sure not one judgmental word would cross her dry, cracking lips.

This one's not a virgin.

That much was obvious as he forced a finger up her from behind. Too loose, even dry. Using the blood from her face as lubricant, two of Jack's finger went into Sam's asshole with some resistance. He wanted to be the first. Finally, a whimper out of the bitch.

As he forced his cock inside her, Jack looked up at the TV. "30 Minute Meals." It took Rachel Ray 30 minutes. It only took him eight.

With his hands around her throat, Sam gave up without a fight just before he came.

There's something to be said for a girl dying on your cock. All her muscles clenching up, shit and blood forcing its way out, it gives you a feeling of accomplishment. Identity.

* * *

Sex has a wonderful effect on getting rid of hangovers. So does a bit of violence. Anything that gets the adrenaline up and the blood flowing, so to speak.

As he lit a cigarette, made his way through lunchtime traffic and down to Mikey's place, Jack felt better. Refreshed. Ready for another drag of a day and another chance to play the kind of person he'd been for a long time now, the crime no longer petty and the malevolence inside him becoming more and more of a constant state.

Mikey was waiting on the stoop like every other afternoon, his nose crusted over from allergies and the occasional coke binge, halfway through a six-pack already.

* * *

Poor Mikey, misguided, his rage misdirected and always out of fashion. A film school dropout and occasional extra or grip on the set, he paid his limited bills by making amateur bondage porn for low-rent websites and jerking off for closet fags at the posh hotels uptown. He liked to think his "films" had some artistic quality, a message about sexual liberation, but really they were just tapes of local slags, out-of-work B-movie actresses and that pathetic lot that Mikey hung around with.

He was always giving me VHS tapes of his latest work—the fucker wouldn't even pony up for a DVD burner—but I could barely get it up for that crap, even with the femdom and fisting scenes. The first night I met Mikey he gave me a tape, and soaring on amphetamines, I managed to squeeze out a pathetic load through my half-limp cock. But ever since then, I've just put the tapes in the drop boxes of local libraries and schools.

Despite his flaws, Mikey's solid enough, though. He's always been there when you need a line or two or to borrow sex toys, no questions asked.

Yeah he's solid enough, he just needs some direction. Some help breaking out of being typecast. This is where I can help him. Where the project can help him.

* * *

Mikey got in the car with a thin smile showing beneath his bloodshot eyes and sad attempt at facial hair.

"Couldn't sleep last night," he said by way of explaining the bags under his eyes, even though they remained a permanent fixture—along with that schoolboy grin—on his sunken, acne-scarred face.

In fact, Mikey had been up until almost dawn with some Section 8 junkie cunt doing rails of crushed up Adderall and heavily stomped on coke, while sexually experimenting on her with various kitchen utensils. In the end, he wound up with almost six hours of raw footage and one hell of a headache. A small price to pay for art.

"I bet you couldn't," Jack said through a smirk. He had seen the greasy bitch watching out the window as he pulled up and the smell of rotten Eastern European pussy permeated from his passenger's clothes and sweat. "Don't you ever get sick of that same old shit night after night?"

"Eh…it's something to do," Mikey sounded bored. "It pays the bills and I get my nut."

"Yeah, but when you've eaten your cereal with the same mixing spoon that explored that infected bitch's birth canal last night, what's left? Where can you go from there?"

"The clinic." Mikey smiled, but as he played back all the scenarios and fluids sloshing around in his head, he wondered if maybe Jack had a point. Maybe you needed something to look forward to. That or maybe you just needed to rethink your boundaries.

As Jack pulled past a bus stop he could feel the eyes following him, but his thoughts drifted to his passenger and his plans for the project.

Mikey was definitely solid. He was just about ready, he just needed to test the waters, feel the strange way that fear made you powerful and violence cleansed you of imposed doubts. It was almost time to begin.

Jack smiled at a young mother waiting for the number nine bus, as he turned left and headed toward today's shooting location. Today he would be "Second Mugger." Tonight he would be something far more interesting.

Chapter Two

Ineffectual degeneracy, some of the inclusions became apparent from loneliness with Mikey's afflictions. Although Jack cared for none of them, much like the sperm-filled friend he was, he opened his eyes in the same way Mikey always did, both at the same time and fully adjusted to darkness.

When Jack started his sexcapades to replace the desire of his past—which was nothing more then spent dreams, ejaculated from his mind into the cesspool of loathsome depravation—he always carried with them a sense of well being. Sure, he could've won an Oscar. Sure, he could've won Golden Globes, always playing a monster. In the most literal sense, he had even played Dracula once. But now he became the ultimate villain, the secret tyrant who lived quietly among the social conglomerate of fashion and Paris Hilton scowls that blindsided the American public, while military action stymied and politicians masturbated to the blood being spilled and the campaign contributions of special interests.

It was no different here, a point to be made. An insurrection. If Jack had to make these films to prove a point, so be it. Plus they were fun. He loved hurting women. He could hear his cunt of a foster mother in every whimper of every bitch he sodomized. Once, when he made a girl swallow eleven bags of skittles and then forced his cock down her throat until she vomited, he made bets with Mikey on which color would come up first. Now, he was making art, or at least recreating the rawest aspects of reality.

Along the rain-drenched alleyway, puddles were ignored and concrete flowers were run over by the worn wheels of the recently resurrected GTO. He still had a few dollars in his bank account, but nothing to start anything major. He had an idea though, he had plans, and sometimes that's all it took.

Dropping the car into low gear, Jack rounded the corner of the alley as Mikey lit a cigarette.

"What was it like being a movie star?"

"You were in movies too. I was never a fucking star," Jack said. "We go over this every week. Why do you want to know so much? That's over now. I don't think about it, and I sure as fuck don't dream about what could have been."

"What do you dream about?" Mikey asked.

"I dream about running this business. I dream about mandatory nationwide abortion. I dream about impaling the president on the American flag. I dream about bombing the universe. Last night I dreamt about those two twins again."

"The twin girls?"

"No the twin towers...yes, the twin girls you fucking dolt," Jack said. "Majora and Manora I call them. I don't know their names, and to tell you the truth, I don't care, but Majora is a redhead and Manora has the darkest fucking hair you can imagine, with strips of Smurf blue through it. I ordered a ball gag to match that fucking hair of hers."

"Why do you keep dreaming about them?"

"I don't know...last night they were eating each other raw, and I was fucking Majora up the ass while my head was in a noose. I wanted to fall off the bed. I wanted her to move out of the way and go right off the bed, so I could dangle. You know they say you have the most powerful erection when you hang yourself, and when I get to hell, I'm going to find Marilyn Monroe and see if her pussy is as wet as JFK remembers it."

"What the fuck are you on about?" Mike asked, tilting back a pint of gut-rot whiskey as they continued down the alley, and where the fuck are we going?"

"To find a star."

Mike looked at Jack and laughed, as the sun behind them became a bloody orange and the autumn was just right for change.

* * *

"I want to watch a horror movie the next time I'm fucking," Mikey broke the short silence.

"You *are* a horror movie, Mikey," Jack laughed, pulling up to an embankment just outside the city limits.

"What are we doing?" Mikey asked. "I thought we were going to find an actress."

"What do you think is funding this fucking business? We need cash my man." Jack threw Mikey a rubber George W. Bush mask. "Here, put it on and try not to kill anyone."

"We're going to rob a Mexican restaurant?" Mikey asked, looking up at the pastel colors and burnt out neon Corona signs.

"Yeah, banks are too dangerous and Mexicans never report shit anyway." Jack exited the car, tossing Mikey a 9mm Luger. He was wearing long sleeves covering his tattoos. They cut through the trees and waited for a lull in traffic.

"Remember, don't kill anyone, we don't need a death on our hands," Jack said.

What about the two girls from last night? Isn't their blood on your hands? Rich cunts don't really count do they?

Jack looked down at the scars on his right palm, thinking about his foster mother, then he pulled on leather gloves. The last thing to go on was the rubber Reagan mask.

"Let's rob the new America," he whispered as they ran across the alley and stooped down to go through the back. Mikey kept the safety off on his pistol even though he would never use it. He was told not to kill anyone and he couldn't even if he wanted to.

"This is it."

"Jesus, Jack, I don't know if…"

"You want to be a broke nobody forever?"

"No sir, Dutch."

"Then shut the fuck up and hold on… 'It's time to choose'," Jack smiled. "Time to pull ourselves up by the bootstraps."

The back door of the Testa Tequa smashed inward, making the three fry cooks in the kitchen hesitate. Two men rushed in wearing masks, guns drawn. No one moved, and no one screamed, not until Jack pointed the Glock at the makeshift stage and shot a mariachi musician in the face.

"Christ!" Mikey screamed. The guitar player twisted and fell, blood spraying from the corner of his head in freshets.

"I thought you said not to kill anyone!"

"I did," Jack whispered. "I guess he forgot to duck."

Moving quickly towards the middle of the dining area, Jack pointed the gun at a group of patrons.

"Alright. I think you've seen enough movies to know how this goes… I want to see those fucking wallets."

Jack pointed at the guitar player still twitching on the stage, blood gargling out of his mouth. "I had to prove a point. Don't make me prove another."

Mikey looked at Jack, still in shock.

Wallets came out, and Jack collected them, just as a twenty-something woman stood from her stool, nine months pregnant, a puddle of amniotic fluid forming below her.

"Shit!" Mikey said. "Ronnie!"

Jack glanced in the direction of the bar.

"I think this bitch's water broke."

Jack looked at her, as she stood with her mouth yawning in mid-scream, her eyes frozen in terror. Jack approached slowly, gun at his side.

"Now I just bet you're not at all worried that I'm going to shoot you…are you preggo?"

"Please…" the woman, a local nurse named Wendy Miller, squeaked. "Please. I didn't do anything."

"Maybe I was wrong."

"Please don't…"

Jack came closer, drawing his gun as Mikey made himself busy collecting the rest of the wallets. "Would you stop fucking around? Let's not turn this into Tehran."

Jack lowered his head, resting his mask-covered face up against Wendy's bulging belly.

"I bet it's a boy…am I right, mom?"

"Ye…ye...yes," Wendy whispered.

"You think your son has a chance in this world? Maybe I should do you a favor and blow his brains out through your ass? Why…I bet he'd probably strangle himself with his umbilical cord right now if he knew what life turned out to be."

"What?" Wendy sobbed as Jack pulled the hammer back on the pistol and pressed the barrel against her stomach.

"I begged my foster mother to kill *me* when I was younger, but she never did. Instead she'd peel my fingernails off when I bit them. Beat me for not being a girl. Piss in a glass and make me drink it when I wet the bed."

Jack pulled the glove back off his right hand, holding out a scarred palm "See that?

"When I was bad, when I forgot to pick up toys, or help her, she used to make homemade horror movies…no cameras. Those are the ones I remember the clearest. She used to iron clothes for dad before he'd go to work, and every once in a while, she'd mistake my hand for his shirts.

When she died, I was glad, it meant there was no more ironing."

Wendy said nothing, mascara tears trailing.

"I'm going to do *your* son a favor."

The gun went off and Wendy's mouth went slack as she fell backward onto a dirty aquarium with sickly tropical fish inside. Glass and saltwater went everywhere. Her baby never took a breath outside the womb.

"So much for a woman's right to choose," Mikey dropped a wallet, his face blank under the mask.

Jack ran and snatched up the rest of the cash.

"Alright, Georgie! Time to get rolling before Feingold shows up."

"Way ahead of you," Mikey said, taking a minute to pull himself together before stepping over Wendy's body and heading back out through the kitchen. In the distance, sirens sounded, but by the time Jack and Mikey had stripped off the masks, changed clothes and headed out, that was only an afterthought.

"Jesus that was fun!" Jack laughed as he gunned the car forward into what was turning out to be a ridiculously humid afternoon.

Mikey sat in shock.

"What's the matter Mikey? Too much for you?"

"I can't believe you fucking shot her."

"It's easy, just point and shoot."

Mikey said nothing.

"You know, when I had the gun pressed up against her stomach I had a hard-on.... and when I pulled the trigger...well...it's no wonder I changed pants."

The Pontiac rolled up the highway at an easy sixty miles an hour, and with the sirens still fading in the distance, Jack swung onto a back road and spun into the loose gravel parking lot of a rundown animal shelter.

No wonder everyone ends up in the suburbs.

* * *

"Wait here."

"Why?"

"Because we don't need anyone getting suspicious. The cops will be looking for two guys, and if they question anyone in here they'll say they saw both of us."

Walking from the car, Jack made his way into the shelter and strode up to the front desk. The place stunk of animal piss, with a tang of spoiled food. A young girl stood behind the desk in a stained white smock. Jack imagined her wearing it while he carved his name into her bald pussy with a bottle opener.

"Hello."

"Hi there," Jack said. "I'm looking for a few good dogs."

"What kind of dogs?"

"Something with nice teeth."

The woman hesitated, but waved Jack toward a row of kennels in the next room.

"The name's John," he said, not finding any security cameras in a quick study of the lobby. "What's yours if you don't mind me making conversation?"

"Heather."

Jack held out his hand. Heather shook it.

"You're a beautiful woman, Heather, ever thought about going into the film industry?"

"Is that where you work?"

"Don't we all? Aren't we just living out one big movie right now?" Jack looked up at the ceiling; his gray eyes the color of asylum steps.

"This is all just a movie," he lowered his face back down to Heather, smiling.

Heather liked his smile, but at the same time found something wrong with it.

"But yeah, I do work in the industry."

"What kind of movies do you make?" Heather asked.

The dogs began to growl and bark as Heather leaned against an empty cage.

"The kind that can make you a star."

"I think you'd better leave. There're cameras in here." Heather was obviously nervous now.

"No there aren't," Jack smiled again, "but I can take you to a place where there are all *sorts* of cameras…and we can make movies…we can make art, *bitch*."

Heather's eyes widened, right before Jack slugged her in the stomach and drove her head into a wooden beam between kennels. She went limp and the screaming dogs went crazy in their cages.

Mikey was drumming on the dashboard when Jack came out dragging something in a white sheet, two pit bulls in tow. When he saw the dangling arm of a woman, Mikey put his face in his hands and sighed.

"That's not a dog."

"Well, two of them are," Jack smirked.

"You're a piece of work you know that?"

"And the vagina is a fountain of youth," Jack shot back.

"A piece of work and fucking random." Mikey finally cracked a smile.

"It is. The vagina is where a child is born, and what follows an infant from the birth canal? I know in your case, fried eggs since you bang chicks with kitchen utensils, but for the rest of us, the fountain of youth is a woman's vagina. What goes comes out must go in…or something like that…what the fuck was my point?"

"I have no idea."

"Oh, well," Jack started the car, Heather Grier's sleeping body slumped in the backseat. "Let's get young again."

Mikey looked at Jack and watched him laugh as the rear tires tore free of the parking lot.

"Don't we have a movie to make?"

"Yep, and I've got our star."

* * *

Darkness smothered the sunrise as Jack parked near the docks. Exiting the car, hair slicked back, sporting a jean jacket and white t-shirt, he lit a Camel and stood among the empty boat slips. Soon after, a Lincoln Town Car pulled up next to him. Inside was Albertino Torez.

"Get in," Albertino said, "and put out that cigarette."

"So I guess I don't have to worry about a smoking fetish, huh?" Jack laughed. Albertino didn't smile, instead, he waited for Jack to make his way to the side of the car and get in. Jack held out his hand, but Torez did not shake it. He looked at Jack with distain and a scar running deep along his chin.

"You're price is a little high, Mr...?"

"You can call me John...but I don't think you know what the price entails."

"I do, but I can buy snuff films in Mexico for *half* the price."

"Not like these, not personalized, you can't."

Albertino remained quiet, and then sighed. "Still, twenty thousand dollars is..."

"Mr. Torez..." Jack said. He placed a hand on the Guatemalan man's leg. "Do you know twenty thousand dollars is exactly the amount the mafia in Jersey charges to kill someone? The highest number of deaths from any pro in Jersey is eight. Did you know that?"

Torez looked at the hand on his leg, the tattoo on Jack's left hand was dark.

"No," Albertino said.

"I once played a mobster in the movies...quite a few years ago. Guess where I got inspiration?"

"The mafia?" Albertino asked.

"No..." Jack laughed, and his eyes grew bright. "No my friend, I got my inspiration from my left hand."

Albertino read the tattoo on Jack's left hand. It was the tattoo of a number.

"IIIII IIIII".

"That's how many people *I've* killed Albertino...and I got that tattoo when I was 19. So do yourself a favor and don't back out of the deal now. It's twenty thousand, but I'm going to be nice and only ask for half up front."

Albertino reached down between his legs and grabbed the handle of a briefcase. He handed it to Jack without a word.

"Now that that ugly business is out of the way, Mr. Torez, what exactly did you have in mind for the film?"

"I want her to scream," Albertino said. "I...I *like* that."

"Anything else?"

"I want to watch."

"Not a chance. There are rules, Mr. Torez, and I believe I explained that on the phone. Half the money up front, then you get the DVD, then I get the rest of the money."

"You say it like we have a contract," Albertino laughed. "There's no fucking contract, John..."

Suddenly, Jack pulled the Glock from his jacket and placed the barrel against the side of Torez's face.

"*Here* is my contract you spic motherfucker...now...do you want me to *sign* it?"

"No..." Albertino said.

"If you back out of this now, I'll call your wife... I know the 'produce' stand she operates out of on Route 42. Don't think I don't have my ass covered. I'll ruin your life in the blink of an eye. Work with me and everything will be fine, got me?"

"Yes."

Jack lowered the gun.

"I'm a director, not an actor Mr. Torez," Jack got out, but leaned back in the car. "Same place, in three days, same time."

"Fine, just get it done."

"Good man. Don't you worry about that."

Chapter Three

Mikey paced back and forth across the basement of the steadily-deteriorating townhouse he and Jack now called home. He was ready to move on, to take the next step, and lord knew he needed money, but this? Bondage was one thing—it was consensual at least—but rape?

Heather was awake now, tied to a chair in the corner, mumbling something through a ball gag he had designed—another hobby of his—this one clear synthetic rubber with a Sydney funnel-web spider staring out.

Cute wasn't how most people would describe her right now, but it seemed to fit for Mikey. It somehow made the decision easier.

* * *

Fuck it.

* * *

As the anxiety subsided and the idea grew on him, Mikey walked over to Heather, letting his nostrils fill with the odor of cat piss and cleaning chemicals that radiated from her work clothes. He touched her face, tipping her chin up as she recoiled and forced out a muffled "please..."

Despite bringing the smells of the kennel with her, he was getting turned on.

She was thin, with smooth, slightly-freckled skin, dirty blonde hair and full lips stretched thin and pale by the gag.

Mikey grabbed a handful of her hair and pulled her head back, forcing Heather's cleavage out as he started to unbutton her blouse. Then he pulled her floor length, neo-hippie skirt down to her feet, using a folding knife to cut the

23

fabric from around her bound ankles, getting hard as he ripped her panties down. The picture was now complete. As Mikey ran his fingers over the razor bumps around her pussy, he heard the door to the basement open and Jack walk down, two dogs in tow.

"I see you started without me," Jack laughed. "Don't stop on my account."

"Just seeing what we're, getting into." Mikey forced a smile.

"Does it meet your approval?"

"Uhuh."

"And you're okay with this? Ready to create something real?" Jack asked Mikey, ignoring any input Heather might have.

"Yeah...but what the fuck are you doing with the dogs?"

"Let's just call them extras," Jack said, a smile creasing his face as he pulled out a utility knife and started cutting the electrical cord binding Heather to the rusted folding chair.

"Set the camera up over there," Jack pointed to a second chair set up on a white sheet in front of a clean, white-washed wall of aging cinder blocks.

Mikey fastened the MiniDV camcorder to a tripod and angled it at the "set." He flipped on several unfiltered spotlights—the kind you could pick up at any hardware store—and made the white backdrop almost blinding. Mikey didn't know it yet, but it was about to make the perfect canvas.

"Have a seat." Jack smiled at Mikey as he took the ball gag out of Heather's mouth and retied her hands in front of her.

"What are you doing?" she croaked, her throat dry and crackling.

"What we're being paid to do," Jack said, admiring the way the backlighting made him look in the reflection of her eyes.

He knew it was cliché and somewhat out of context, but Jack couldn't help reciting Mickey Knox.

It's just murder. All God's creatures do it. You look in the forests and you see species killing other species, our species killing all species, including the forests, and we just call it industry, not murder.

Mikey looked confused.

* * *

The RECORD light on the camera blinked red and Jack pushed Heather to her knees in front of Mikey, who already had his cock out and hard.

"Suck it like your life depended on it," he laughed as he pushed her face into Mikey's crotch. "We can give you all the motivation you need."

Heather tentatively took the head of the erection glaring at her into her mouth, hoping this was all they wanted. Jack took his position behind the camera, focusing in on the side of her face, tears trickling down her cheeks, mascara running, as her head slowly bobbed up and down. He was careful not to get Mikey's face in the frame.

Mikey took the back of her head, pushing further into her mouth and down her throat.

"Let her do the work," Jack instructed. "Make her earn the starring role."

"She doesn't seem too into it," Mikey said, with a hint of something that would have resembled guilt if Jack didn't know better.

"She will be," Jack walked over to the basement stairs where he'd tied up the two pitbulls.

Leading the dogs over to Heather, he took the muzzles off them, holding onto their leashes with one hand

and pulling her back by the hair with his other. She coughed, a stream of spit and mucus spilling down her chin.

Mikey looked as concerned as her.

"I'm going to make this as simple as possible," Jack told Heather. "He comes, I call off the dogs."

"What…what are you…" Heather choked out.

With that, he pushed her forward and unlatched the pitbulls from their restraints. The dogs lunged forward, one clamping on her calf muscle as the other snapped down on her left breast, taking the nipple off cleanly and swallowing it.

Heather let out a scream that was immediately muffled as she pushed her head back down on Mikey's cock, choking and stretching her mouth as wide as she could. As one of the dogs continued to tear the muscle out of the back of her leg, Heather threw up, stomach bile, blood, and the vegetable soup she had for lunch dribbling down Mikey's balls. The warmth made him thrust deeper into her throat and he shot a ropey, guilt-filled load inside her swollen mouth.

Heather pulled back.

"Call them off," she croaked.

Jack laughed, and one of the pitbulls latched onto her neck. The dog's teeth pulling out her throat, and Heather dropped to the blood-soaked sheet and twisted her face as her eyes rolled back into her head. Her last breath escaped through the gash in her jugular as Mikey's come bubbled out behind it.

"Cut."

Chapter Four

The first step was always the hardest, but Mikey had made it through. Not as much could be said for Heather, but free enterprise wasn't always free. As new projects rolled in, it got easier, at times enjoyable, and most importantly, profitable. The focus was on art...well, art *and* money ...well, mostly money, but there was something to be said for the way children would drool blood when you lazily pushed a knife into their lungs or the look on a girl's face when she realized she no longer had eyelids.

Eventually, Jack and Mikey stopped looking for outside jobs; they all but moved into a dilapidated townhouse and built a basement studio and impressive client list.

The requests were varied—sometimes extreme and other times quaint by the standards of their current industry—but the rules were simple.

No last names. No watching. Cash only.

You got one copy of an unmarked DVD-R. What you did with it from there was up to you.

Cash for one fantasy.

End transaction.

* * *

"So what's next?" Mikey asked from a ratty couch in the corner, tipping back the last of the morning's first can of stout.

"We wait," Jack answered, lighting a cigarette and glancing at the computer screen in front of him. He was editing last night's work and laughed half-heartedly as the audio playback came through the desktop speakers.

The girl was a whore from across town, about 19-years-old, skinny, greasy. They couldn't find a non-professional matching what the client wanted. So here she was, a recent amateur slut turned pro, looking to keep a needle in her arm and formula in her baby's belly— in that order. Wearing construction boots and a tool belt, she was tied ass-up over a sawhorse. Some contractor's wet dream, she looked up at the camera.

"I can't believe I'm letting you do this," she said from behind a not-so-sheepish smile.

"Me either," a masked Mikey answered as he switched on an electric drill and started toward her spread twat.

As blood and small chunks of her labia splattered against the lens, she let out a cry and Jack pushed "BURN" at the bottom of the editing software window on the screen. Turing the volume off, he looked at Mikey.

"Suppose we should clean up from last night."

"I hate that part."

"Hey, nobody said running a business was going to be easy."

"Yeah, yeah." Mikey rolled off the couch, threw the empty beer can at a trashcan across the basement and picked up a pair of rubber dish gloves. "Let's get this over with."

Using a pair of hacksaws to cut what was left of the nameless girl into smaller pieces, the two of them then pulled the corners of the tarp together and tied it off with the same electrical cord they had used to tie her to the sawhorse.

Waste not want not.

"At least this guy didn't want a fatty," Mikey said as he threw the bundle over his shoulder and started toward the back basement stairs that led to a small, stand-alone garage. "We've really got to start charging more for that."

"Do you think people would pay specialty fees for snuff porn," Jack wondered out loud.

"What other choice do they have? It's not like they can go to fucking Blockbuster for this shit."

Jack laughed.

"The only thing better than a pervert is a pervert with money."

The computer beeped and the tray from the DVD burner slid out.

A quick, high-temperature burning, a cooler with a few bricks and a nice large body of water.

Money in the fucking bank.

* * *

Jack and Mikey returned a few hours later, their cargo gone and the DVD in the hands of its new owner.

Opening a small, fire-proof safe that was stowed under the couch, Jack threw a new crisp bundle of bills inside and latched the top, tossing a key back to Mikey, who had already opened another beer and turned on the shitty old TV set resting on a milk crate in the corner.

"You know, maybe it's time we did a little shopping; a new TV, some furniture, equipment..."

"Shut the fuck up. There's something coming on," Mikey pointed at the screen and turned the volume up.

It was a report on the local news. Authorities were still looking for leads in the disappearance of Heather Grier, a vet tech at the East Side Animal Shelter, the Katie Couric wannabe behind the news desk chirped, a little too happy to be on the air. It had been almost two and a half weeks since she was reported missing and there was no real update.

There was nothing about the second or third girls or last night's star. The police and news folks hadn't connected the two missing children from uptown with Heather yet. Even when they found the bodies, the manner of death and lack of DNA would probably keep them from putting two and two together. Heather died from dog bites, the kids from hundreds of knife wounds and eventually a foot-long blade through their ribcages. The girl had lost it when she saw her brother die. Her screaming was horrific, but that film brought in double the cash.

"So far so good," Mikey said.

"Don't get cocky," Jack shot back. "Just keep it simple and detached. Be careful and keep your mouth shut."

* * *

And therein lays the problem. You can't tell anybody what you're doing, but you've got to have buyers to make any cash. A fucking Catch-22. At least Mikey's coming into his own, taking the lead on some shoots. Showing a little fucking creativity. He even seems to be enjoying himself most of the time. Get a nut; get some quick bank, who could blame him?

Not to worry, though, no more playing rapists and murders in shitty straight-to-video thrillers and true crime bio pics, no more being watched. Only living out other people's fantasies. Doing what they think about when they fuck their wives or mistresses or daughters or whatever they're putting their dicks in this week. Anyway, it's my turn to judge.

The phone hasn't rang in two days. Maybe we'll finally get a couple nights off to go out and enjoy the money that's been piling up too fast to spend.

* * *

As the sun set through the blinds covering the ground-level windows of the basement, Mikey tossed another can onto the pile growing near the trashcan.

"I'm bored," he said, looking over at Jack who had nodded off in a recliner near the TV. "And hungry."

"So eat something…and go jerk off."

"I've already done that twice today."

"Eaten?"

"No."

"So what do you want to do?"

And there was another problem. What did you do for fun when you could live out your most twisted desires at work?

"I don't know, man, want to go bowling?"

Part II:
History Repeating

Chapter Five

When Jack Sanders was sixteen he tried to kill himself.

He was unsuccessful but learned later that the neighbor girl, Betty Broloski succeeded where he failed.

Still a child in every emotional sense, Jack tried to imagine what it must've felt like putting the barrel of a gun in his mouth like she had. He tried to imagine how the gun oil would taste—bitter and greasy.

The thought of walking into the local five and dime and purchasing the oil for such an occasion warmed his judgment. His shaky thumbs pulling the trigger slowly back. Jack wasn't the brave soul Betty was. She didn't think about it, she just did it. She hit rock bottom and pulled the trigger. Simple as that.

How would that little notch at the end of the barrel feel on the end of Jack's tongue? Would he know exactly when the slug pushed through the back of his head? Would he lie dying like Betty did, trying to get up, slipping in her own blood.

The bullet hadn't killed her immediately. It exited through the side of her face, and the cops found her left eye in one of her mother's azalea plants on the kitchen counter. They found her handprints everywhere—most of them on the smooth refrigerator door. During that hot July afternoon, her blood had coagulated like jelly on the vinyl floors. Jack remembered his foster father recounting the details years later when he and his brother visited him at Moore House Chapel Asylum.

* * *

For Betty it was a summer of freedom, and I was her unknown prodigy, still searching for autonomy.

Ever since then, I've tried to live in freedom, but it's been a lie up until now. We all have to pay taxes, fulfill corporate-created needs and answer to our instilled conscience. We read the papers, feign outrage and fuck on our anniversaries. If everyone in the world committed suicide, where would all the politicians go and what would be left to own? They call freedom the American dream, but it's because you have to be asleep to believe it. How many people have died for freedom? No one likes to talk about that, except to justify sacrificing more lives for the bottom line.

Everyone has a name and a story to tell. What I remember is the instance, the changing of perspective, whether by chance or circumstance.

I tried to kill myself on a Friday, twenty years ago. The same night Betty was outside on her swing set. The night before she killed herself and saved my life. Just like a raindrop, I was born to fall. The woman who gave birth to me was high on cocaine in the delivery room. I don't remember it, but people say she was a whore. My biological father had some secrets of his own.

* * *

Jack had never really called the dogs off of Heather. Truth be told, her never intended to. He had seen it played out before.

* * *

My earliest memory was of my foster mother lighting her candles all around the house while dad played his 78s on granddad's Victrola. My foster father was born in the same small Pennsylvania town where I was raised, in a hospital that now highlights an annual haunted house tour. Our basement should have been featured on that tour. All that candle wax.

My foster father was a well-respected man despite his inner loneliness and obvious demons. I always understood him in a way, though. Probably because of what my foster mother did to us both.

It's healthy to embrace fantasy. The darker, the more an answer is found for each of them. People tend to run too quickly for help. The answers are all in your questions, in your darkness. Save your money, put the wallet away.

I stayed alone through most of my childhood.

* * *

Despite being abused since the day he came home from the maternity ward, Jack wasn't a depressed child. He kept to himself outside of school, but loved music and constantly carried a Kinoflex Super 8 camera with him, filming everything from kids playing kickball to dogs giving birth. Music was his first form of expression, then acting. Now, he had a new enterprise.

And with his foster mom…well…hanging from a basement rafter is another form of expression.

* * *

Christmas that year was unseasonably warm. It had been two weeks since her little sister had found Betty when I slipped the rope around my foster mother's neck and kicked the chair she used to tie me to out from under her.

The local paper had called it the "start of an epidemic."

I remember her biting her tongue in two when the rope tightened. I remember the sound of her house slipper falling off her foot and smacking the concrete floor. I remember her eyes bulging out from their sockets and the windows behind them drawing dark like curtains. Exploding colors of synapses and loss of circulation. All those years she had choked me, now it was her fucking turn. The feel of that rope cutting her off from the world, as her mind separated from her flailing. She pissed blood and shit herself.

That final hush is the same as the one you're born with. We're brought into this world with that hush, that last moment of peace before the screaming starts.

I remember the hard-on forming at the thought of my dead mother, toes pointing at the floor. It was still there when the paramedics came to cut her down.

* * *

Jack awoke that night after dreaming of Heather's performance. He had thought of his foster mother when he looked into her eyes and heard the dogs. She had Melanie Sanders' eyes.

* * *

I passed out after my mother spit her last breath. First the paramedics showed up. Then the neighbors. Everyone assumed I found her that way. Everyone was polite enough not to ask about my hard-on. I remember the taste of cinnamon chewing gum in my mouth. The paramedic must have been chewing it. It's the odium that brought me back to life from a tunnel of what should have been guilt. I didn't see any light, but I wanted to go towards it just the same.

* * *

After years of mediocrity, Jack felt like he had truly made something of himself in the film business. Sure, there were no credits, but the money was starting to roll in and he was creating something real.

Those little things about his foster mother, he would cherish them forever. Force them through in every new project. Like how she used to make the best peanut butter and jelly sandwiches and would take Jack to the park because his father was too busy. How she used to clip off the tips of the cherry flavored freezer pops. How she used to come into his bedroom while he slept and gag him before she sodomized him with a wire coat hanger.

She always said I deserved to feel the pain she felt.

After Betty, the only friend Jack had was his dog Strada. That dog went everywhere with him.

Jack got out of bed, walked to the sliding door of his room and watched as the clouds grew dark and brutal. It always made him feel small.

* * *

I knew then how dark places could get. Even with the lights off and the depth of midnight creeping in, black is not truly black until you've come to terms with death.

I passed out that day and my life hasn't been the same since. I came back to the sounds of hospital monitors, the stench of antiseptic and the glare of white walls. I spent the next few days in the hospital and a week or so under constant psychiatric evaluation.

I spent the next four years of my life lying to doctors, telling them how much I missed my foster mom, but I went to bed every night thinking of the next time I'd feel that alive.

The rope is where it all began.

Jack poured himself a drink, blood still drying on his cuticles. The whiskey was smooth and strong, and the relief—although temporary—came in small, sweeping waves. He closed his eyes, lit a cigarette and thought back.

Back to being an actor. Back to being a child.

Every aspiring artist has definitive techniques in style and how they achieve ideas. After I killed my foster mother, I realized I should've been filming it, but it goes back even further than that.

When I was younger, my dog was the fine line of ingenuity and insanity. No one would believe a black mastiff was the origin of memories still haunting me. It all started there and ended with Heather. Everyone has a focal point in their life. Mine happened to be Strada.

* * *

It was a biting November morning, six months after Melanie Sanders died, six months after he found the right victim.

The wind screeched between rock formations at the edge of the woods and Jack whispered a prayer. It took all his strength to respond to his father.

"You have to do it ...I can't." Jack let his 16-year-old eyes wander beyond the dirty dishes stacked on the kitchen counter. The sliding glass door showed it clearly. The family dog, his mastiff, the color of midnight, lay on his side breathing rapidly. Jack was on the verge of tears for the past week as Strada started acting strange.

He lowered his face and turned away from his father long enough to let a tear run down his face and wipe it clean. To Ronald Sanders, a man crying was not a man, he was nothing but a boy, regardless of age. But a tear dribbled down his cheek anyway. The sight was a sinister sentiment.

Before he died, Strada had sat at the door waiting for Melanie to come home. Sometimes he whined for hours, and when Melanie lay down in bed, Strada would sit by her, his massive girth casting shadows among old papered walls. Strada was too forgiving. In the summer, when it grew hot and the dog was in better health, he would walk alongside David and Jack panting from the impenetrable heat of the dense woods. Jack would take Strada with him every summer on the bridge of East Long Branch, and while he fished from the bridge, the dog would wait anxiously for the catch. Now, Strada was on the porch, unable to stand, just panting heavily, his breathing rigid. Every so often he would lift his head above his shoulders to look around.

Birds singing, flying away for winter.

What was left of the October leaves danced around the porch as if a ceremony were being held rather than a funeral. Strada was old in this young world—at least 15 years of age. Death is always expected, but when it comes knocking, no one wants to answer.

"I…I can't, dad."

"Fucking do it!" his father screamed, as Jack saw the tears finally fall from his father's barren face, pocked with age and scars.

"This is part of being a man, son," Ronald Sanders said. "The hardest thing in the world is sometimes the best thing to do. You know how I feel about vets."

Looking toward the dining room foyer, Jack saw the gun cabinet, the wood-stained, glass-covered oak cell. It called out to him like the rafter where his foster mother had swung. In it, seven rifles stood like soldiers, always waiting, always ready. The rifle he picked was the one his father taught him how to shoot with.

"Which one?" Jack asked, his palms sweaty. He didn't know what else he could do. Looking over his father's shoulder, he saw Strada move her front paw in a shiver.

"Shotgun…all the way to the left," his father said.

A vet said two years ago Strada wouldn't make it another three months, but they weren't talking about just any dog. They were talking about the *god* of dogs: Strada. He would die weighing a pinch over two hundred pounds and standing almost four feet tall.

His teeth though, now they were something.

Jack ventured slowly toward the gun cabinet. Taking his time seemed ill-fated, but his mind was trapped. He rubbed his cold hands across his flattop, what dad called an *All-American* haircut and grimaced at his reflection in the glass. The house was as murky as the local pond, and in his reflection, he observed an old man never able to forgive himself for what had to be done. Other kids Jack's age didn't have to do this. Other little boys didn't get blowjobs from their own mother, while a knife was held to their hardly budding balls. Other kids wouldn't be able to handle what Jack was able to handle either, and in a desperate way, that was satisfying.

The cabinet opened, oiled doors completing its silence. The shotgun stood all the way to the left, poised and ready to put things to sleep forever.

Trembling, Jack grabbed the 12-guage pump shotgun from the rack and pulled it free of its lock bonds. The weight of it in his hands made it seem so real, *feel* so real.

"Load it," his foster father steadied his voice, as Jack struggled to hold onto the gun. His voice was strong and frightening in the dimly lit house.

Jack wanted to place the barrel in his mouth and pull the trigger so he wouldn't have to go through with it. That way when the forensic detectives came and picked his teeth and brains off the floor, piece by bloody piece, he'd know his father did it after all.

Strada barked.

Moving faster, Jack loaded three rounds, one was all he needed.

"Hurry up, Jack!" Ronald barked. "He's suffering!"

"I'm trying."

Lowering the shotgun, he breathed deep, closed his eyes and hoped his father didn't see him. He would've snapped for sure. Old Ronald would scream that he was taking too much time, fucking around while their *other* son was lying in pain outside. How selfish could he be? The least he could do was end it fast. Those endless nights protecting them, standing by the front door waiting for them to come home, standing by his bed or sleeping on it while Jack suffered another nightmare.

These days, Jack dreamt *carefully*.

All those days and nights by his foster mom's side shielding her while her mind was eaten away. At 5-years-old, sitting in the summer room, coloring in the face of the Incredible Hulk with a dozen or so crayons. Strada watching him as shadows fell over his shoulder. It was nearing noon, time for soap operas. Except Jack's foster mom didn't watch soap operas. Jack's mom made movies without any cameras.

Strada was there when she died. He barked, whined and cried, even growled, pissed he couldn't save her life. Strada was so big and strong he chased nightmares away. But disease isn't easily frightened, and there he lay—dying.

When Jack reappeared in the kitchen with his father's shotgun, he saw his dad standing by the sliding door, looking out at Strada as if he was a display at a museum rather than a beloved member of the family. All those times he would throw Strada his green ball and Strada would fetch, lumbering back for Jack to throw it again.

"You ready?" Ronald Sanders asked.

He didn't turn around, just lifted his head. At the same time, Strada shook, winced and let out a painful howl.

Where's Dave? Jack remembered thinking. *This was his dog too; he could've taken off work.*

Jack wanted to stall long enough for his brother to help end this tragedy.

The sliding glass door to the back porch slid open.

"Come on," his dad said.

No emotion in his voice, no turning back. Relentless when needed. This was Ronald Sanders.

"Is the safety off?"

Jack looked down at the trigger guard, saw it was, and moved closer to the door. He stepped out into the November morning, both of their jackets off. Dad was shirtless, Jack in a t-shirt. Neither of them dared comment on how cold it was or that they needed coats. Strada was suffering, and what made matters worse, animals couldn't speak to say how appalling it really was. This dog didn't have to…to…

To tell us that he wanted to die. Maybe not all of it was arthritis. Maybe he was afraid of knowing the truth. The only witness to me hanging my foster mother wanting to die with that secret.

"Shouldn't we dig the hole first?" I asked.

Dad turned and faced me, eyes filled with 50 years of tears waiting to fall.

"After. I don't want Strada in more pain then he's already in. After we're done, we'll bury him beside the black oak."

A sudden thought of horror hit me, what if I was unable to lift the dog with my dad and carry him to an open grave?

"Come on..." dad said, pointing at the shotgun in my hand "No time like the present."

Moving cautiously, I raised the shotgun with the stock tight against my shoulder. Terrified, I took aim, trying to remain in the mindset where my foster mother taught me to live. Later in life it would come much easier. 'Shoot first and ask questions later' had always been his cliché' motto when I used to go to the Alibaton quarry in Lauderdale with Strada and Dave. It took years before I was brave enough to jump from the 30-foot cliff into the manmade pond below. When you go to jump, don't think about it, just do it.

Don't worry about hitting the rock-laden bottom; don't worry about the fall, just let go. I finally did it when I was eleven. During football games I didn't worry about getting hurt. I didn't worry about hitting rock bottom. I loved the pain. I worried about winning. In dating, I didn't worry about what to say, I just said it. I didn't worry about how to kiss I just did it. I didn't worry about coming down a girl's leg, or biting her tits till the blood tasted like the answers I'd been searching for. I just did it.

I placed the muzzle of the shotgun against my dog's head. It was like having to kill my brother. I thought briefly about all our times together. Strada looked up from the corner of his eye, as if he knew who was holding the gun, and in the most inhuman way, he looked more human than anyone I've ever known. Tears fell. The birds stopped singing, and in the distance, I could hear my own heartbeat. Time fell on a branch and hung there like a dead man. Everything moved in slow motion. It seemed silly telling a dog I love you, but I did, even in front of my dad. Then I pulled the trigger and hit rock bottom...

* * *

In a brief, cataclysmic second of terror, the gun fired off the shell with an eardrum bursting rhythm. It was like the world exploded for me. Across the horizon, a murder of crows flew south.

I saw what the gun did to my dog but didn't believe it. If I were able to dictate words on paper for a script I would never tell this story alone.

Strada's face tore open; the top of his head blew off in bone shrapnel. Blood flew out in thick, stringy streams, some of it peppering dad's bare chest. Strada reared in a howl of pain. In the last second, when I pulled the trigger on the twelve gauge, I didn't know I missed the center of his head.

Falling to my knees, I sat in shock, my dog lying in pools of blood, fountains of it pouring from its mouth in freshets. His one teddy bear brown eye hung like a dead tadpole on his cheek. Strada was still alive—shaking, shivering, and barking. I watched my only true friend in the world suffer.

Did he know? Did Strada know I missed? Did Strada know I fucked up? Did Strada even know I pulled the trigger?

I let out a burst of tears. Through my grimy vision, I saw the bloody nightmare before me, and through an echo, I heard my father screaming.

"Shoot him again!"

Then, as if in some vicious horror film, Strada lifted his head, shaking, his bloody maw stretched open, and something came out of his throat that resembled a liver. Clotted blood from his brain and what had been left of it hung loosely like his eye. I'd never throw the ball with him again.

The gun was ripped from my hands. My first thought was that my father grabbed the gun to finish off the dog, and I hoped once he was done he would shoot me. I didn't want to live with memories like this serving my dreams. But it was my brother David that grabbed the gun, and in a flurry of spontaneous speed, shot Strada in the head, once, twice, and then done.

* * *

I saw my second of many psychiatrists then. There on the couch again, across from a short, stubby man named Carl. A few weeks without drugs were healing for my conscience. I had nightmares about my dog. It would still be several years before I began searching for acting gigs, ten years before I would be offered a starring role in a major horror film. Carl Sinclair, lollipop in mouth, advised me that every time I had violent thoughts I should write them down on paper and put them in a box. I guess his therapy didn't help, though, because that box is spilling over like the blood that spattered out of Strada's face and the come that bubbled out of Heather's throat.

Chapter Six

The afternoon before Betty offed herself, my brother David was painting an old house on Bursten Street, and there was a report in the Lauderdale Review Ledger *that two teenagers had seen a black dog on the East Long Branch Bridge. No big deal, David thought, until he read the dog was seen walking towards the boys as they fished at night. One even talked about how spooky it was for a summer evening. Fog drifted off the canal like—*

"Ghosts," David said, reading the article aloud to himself. Jack remembered that much. He said that word out loud, and even in the daytime, he believed his own voice.

"Eyewitnesses described the dog as massive and said it walked slowly through the fog on the entrance to the bridge…A Jackie Wilson High School student said the dog had 'glowing red eyes'…also said the closer the dog got to them…there was the smell of gunpowder in the air…"

Lighting a cigarette, David had stood in the sunlight of a new summer. Thinking about the bridge and the accident, he set the paper down on the porch.

Almost two winters ago, when his mom was still alive, David was riding with a friend whose name he now tried to forget. He sat in the passenger's seat listening to Zeppelin and temporarily forgetting the worries of life. It was snowing—the kind of snow that fell in heavy chunks like ashes from the wings of burning angels. His friend pushed the car around a bend on Long Branch Road too fast, and the Pontiac Firebird hit a patch of black ice and spun out at the entrance to the bridge. David's friend was killed instantly. He wasn't wearing his seatbelt and was ejected through the windshield. The skin from his face was found clinging to a frozen tree. David survived, but for the next several months he regretted it.

While the car had drifted sideways, David had braced his body by gripping the roof with one hand. His window was rolled down when the car hit the tree and his hand was still on the roof when the fire department flipped the car back over. David's fingers were intact only by tendrils of skin, bones crushed and flesh stripped like the intestinal casings of sausage. He was in a hospital bed for several weeks after the accident, soaring on painkillers and dazing through the doctors' arguments about whether or not he would lose his fingers.

In the end, they saved his fingers, pinned and cut them open to help the healing process. The doctors kept his hand pinned to a paraffin tray. Jack went to see him every day, listening to him sobbing silently. There is nothing more troubling to a man then another grown man crying. He told the police everything, learned that his friend was killed, and tried to push away the memories of that night.

He was lying on his side, snow peddling down like feathers, his hand trapped under the weight of a car. In the dead of winter, agony burning him, adrenaline pumping, in the distance he heard a dog barking. David remembered thinking about Strada. Turning his head to the left, melting snow freezing his back and the ice cold water burning his bare skin, David thought he saw something near the trees beyond the bend. There was a blotch of darkness. The barking grew louder, closer, more imminent in its persistence. David thought he was losing his mind, because the dog sounded like it was saying his name while it barked. Finally the sound of an approaching car closed in, and through the passing drifts of snow, he saw a black dog smaller then Strada but every bit as mean. He heard a car door open, and the dog drifted closer.

We buried him by the black oak.

Another bark, then David saw a tall skinny kid wearing a Penn State ball cap.

"Are you okay," the kid asked.

"Shoot it," David said as everything went blank.

Chapter Seven

I was fooling myself thinking I could relax when this world had come to a complete halt. Life is full of coincidences, and I didn't mind knowing them. What I did mind was relating to a memory I had been trying to lose for years.

Strada.

I kept the newspaper clippings though...they were like trophies to me...

I killed those three people...I killed them and made it not matter. Because I was young and that was in the past. They were just extras in the movie of my life.

* * *

Jack walked to the shower stall in the bathroom, flipped on the water, waited until it got as hot as the faulty plumbing would allow, and got in.

* * *

You should've killed yourself...

That day should've happened, and you would've been in the ground with all of them, family and friends alike.

In the rendition of time, with every breath, the air grew stale and raging wind pounded against my brother's van like drums. It was the last day of November. We drove all day, past the old trees that were stripped free of their leaves. The newspapers on the dashboard revealed stories about the lives of the missing, the scared and the dead. We drank Turkey Hill iced tea that dad brought back from Pennsylvania, smoked Camel cigarettes and listened to bands from our past, mostly The Clash. I was there that day, remembering it as if I hadn't pulled the trigger, and as the sun went down in the burning glow of tomorrow, I saw the wind die among the lifeless, leaf-littered sidewalks where we'd never walk again.

Dave and I had to know the distance between our nightmares and us.

The graveyard scared me, but not as much as the bridge at the end of the road. Long Branch Road lay barren, and we passed over most of it before butterflies warmed my stomach with a fluttering sickness. We rolled up to the entrance of the bridge, where not even God would venture tonight. Whatever evil walked here, walked alone.

Lights went off; the music was trapped in the void of the van, as I locked all the doors and sat smoking my last cigarette and bottoming out my tea. The fog seemed to drift up onto the bridge like a smoke screen and hover only at the beginning. Glancing over at the newspapers on the passenger's seat, I looked at the front cover of the that day's Ledger. *The above-the-fold headline read* Police Investigating Recent Rash of Murders. *I gulped, lifted the newspaper away to reveal the revolver underneath, took a breath and opened the glove box. This is where the guy killed all his victims, and this is where my brother found out it was me.*

The van door opened with a rusty creak. I stepped out, hands in my coat pockets. I was careful not to move the gun too much. I didn't want to shoot myself in the belly. The bridge looked as though it was cut in half by the fog. Dave and I took three slow steps towards the haze.

"What do you think, bro?"

"I think we're making a mistake," I said.

"Strada," David whispered.

I remember how his voice sounded. It was so real and vivid. More than any movie you could imagine.

"This is the bridge where it all started…where we used to fish…remember?"

"No," I lied.

The sun began to exit in a purple liverish drowning light of a newfound darkness that filled my brother's face with the appearance of deep sorrow.

"I don't want to remember."

On that bridge, I waited for David to turn around and look down off the bridge before I shot him in the back of the head, flipped his body over the side and went back home. I'd like to think he was thinking about our dog, but I don't know. I'm not so sure. In my dreams, he knows I shot him; in fact…he went there that day hoping I would.

* * *

Jack lathered himself with soap in the shower, the water streaming pink down the drain, most of it left over from Heather's torn pussy.

* * *

After these events, I spent most of my free time writing. I tried to block the memories of Strada from my head. I started penning a manuscript about Strada, but I shelved it when I could never find an appropriate ending.

I tried to kill myself again after my foster dad found out David had been murdered. I sat in my first apartment listening to "Suspicious Minds" by Elvis Presley and almost pulled the trigger, thinking about Betty Broloski and knowing that my mother would be waiting for me in hell. She would smile and come running for me, wanting to rake my pants down and begin licking and biting me all over; "Angel Whispers" she called them. She was so high on Vicodin and other pills, it was no wonder she would buy nothing but black licorice and force me to eat it.

So for the first three weeks of my four-month stay at Moorehouse Chapel, I spent my nights strapped down, the walls coated with padded triangle-shaped buttons. I used to imagine those buttons as different colors. White—the neutral color of thought. The buttons became blinking eyes to me. I wanted to kill myself more than ever while I was locked up. I always wondered how so many people spent their days doped up. I was always nauseated from the Methylphenidate they gave me and the doses of saltpeter. The Methylphenidate kept you calm, the saltpeter kept you limp. You never wanted to fuck after ingesting saltpeter. A sad day for me, a safe one for the nurses.

I loved watching men much older than me trying to find answers to why a 17-year-old boy would try to kill himself. My doctors actually looked crazy themselves after the idealistic viewpoints of opinion makers found nothing to eliminate from the questions or even secure why I would do such heinous things to my own body. I was never ashamed of what I did; the only thing I regretted was watching my foster father destroy himself over it. I don't know if I would've done it if I hadn't killed my foster mother. When she died, the life I lived remained empty.

When I was lonely, my foster mother was always in my life, and I knew that. When she died, however, it was over and my days were vacant.

I had regular meetings to go to every week. The kind where everyone with so-called problems would show up and start breathing my perfectly good air. They were the whiners of life, a waste of good amniotic fluid if you asked me. Wherever these ignorant pigs came from should be burned down. I had to suffer for three more years, listening to fat people talk about why they eat until they want to puke. I listened to sluts moan that they can't stop fucking. I listened to all these people tell the group why they cut their wrists and make up bullshit stories. I still believed we we're living in someone else's dreams and were figments of someone else's elapsed past and time. Still, when it came time for me to answer why I put the gun in my mouth, I told the therapist that I didn't know, and that was the truth. I didn't know why, or I didn't really care.

* * *

When I met Tiffany Garish at the meetings, I became someone so different. I never thought anyone would be able to take me away from life like Tiffany could. Of all the things I can't remember, I remember that day in the meeting room. She was sitting there with her legs crossed and her milky skin brightened by the dull fluorescent lights buzzing above. She was wearing a mini skirt, playing with her black hair, and popping pink bubblegum. I remember thinking how good she looked in her black knee-high boots. Her lips were black. For Tiffany, everyday was Halloween.

The next day, she met me outside in the rain. The cars made wet hollow sounds as they drove by, casting the ghostly red of brake lights in the reflections of puddles. I didn't have the nerve to ask her out, but I became nervous for the first time in a long time when she asked me for a cigarette.

"Sure," I said. Shaking one out of a pack, I saw the tattoo on her wrist, the pentagram. "Nice tattoo."

I lit the cigarette. In her eyes the flames made me feel easier.

"It's not a tattoo," she said. "It's a birthmark."

I knew she was lying. The tattoo was black as pen ink. She was just fucking around, but I suppose the smile that followed was her way of letting me know I was welcome in her world.

"You want to see more?" she asked.

Later I fucked her and made her strangle me. I thought about my foster mother and came knowing the case would never be reopened. Later, I'd fuck Tiffany in her ass, greasing it with lard and pouring alum in her cunt. I loved her hands around my throat while I came. I'd fuck her to see the world.

Tiffany took away the murderous tick most of the time. She was the most gorgeous woman in the world. Dark hair, the color of oil before being lit on fire. Dark make-up that slid down her face every so often, especially when she cried. Sometimes I want to go to hell just to see her. She used to let me do the most delicious things, and she made me want to feel that gun in my mouth again. We would stay up at night watching zombie flicks, smoking cigarettes, and drinking blackberry wine.

They found Tiffany walking around aimlessly one day in Wilmington. She snapped shortly after we'd broken up, took a fistful of pills, went drinking at some dive bar, and walked up to a patrolman. While his back was turned, she pulled his service revolver, shot him in the back of the head, dropped the gun right there on the street and kept on walking. The police caught up with her a few blocks later.

* * *

During the years that led up to my move out west, I tried other ways to kill myself, and I felt liberated in a way that was indescribable.

I was untouchable, invincible.
I had purpose.

* * *

Jack's shower was interrupted by the ring of his cell phone. Reaching out to it from the stall, he grabbed it and flipped it open.

"Yeah?"

"Is this John?" the gruff voice asked.

"Maybe. Who's this?"

"A prospective customer."

"Yeah?" Jack said. "How'd you get this number, prospect?"

"A friend of yours."

"I don't have friends."

"We all have friends, John...look, I have a proposition for you."

"Not on the phone you don't," Jack said. "I don't discuss business over the phone."

"Meet me at the Memorial Cemetery off Interstate 101 tonight at nine."

"Who am I meeting?"

"There'll be a white Bentley parked near Roses Pharmacy. I have a possible buyer for one of your films."

"How do you know about my films?"

"Word gets around...I would be happy to discuss it with you then."

"Wait a goddamn minute, I don't just go meeting people I don't know...especially about my work. This isn't a fucking civil service function."

"We have cash waiting for you, John. My boss would like to discuss a business arrangement."

Jack paused. "I'll find you."

"Good enough…"

The phone went dead.

* * *

In an hour, Jack was dressed and having a drink at a bar off the interstate and watching the TV that hung above the rows of bottles.

They were still talking about the robbery at the Mexican restaurant on the local news. A few girls were also reported missing from the area, but the newscaster didn't mention anything about a connection. Meanwhile, Mikey was back in the basement smoking coke and counting the money. He was waiting for Jack and another job, but mostly he was just waiting to get off.

* * *

The cemetery came into view as Jack gunned the car toward the pharmacy and saw the pearl white Bentley idling with its wiper blades moving back and forth. He saw the car's headlights give a few flashes then pull forward as he lined up side by side with the tinted driver's side window of the luxury sedan. The window went down slowly and a man wearing a baseball cap pulled down over his eyes looked up at Jack.

"John, I presume?"

"Yeah."

"Get in the car, we'll take a ride."

"I don't take rides from strangers," Jack smiled.

"Okay," the driver said, turning to the backseat and whispering something.

"Mr. Fairlane wants to know if he can get in your car."

"Alone…and unarmed…and tell Mr. Fairlane I'm *very* armed."

"Fair enough."

The door opened, and a tall man in a trench coat stepped out and hurried through the rain to the passenger's side of the GTO. Jack knew there was someone in the Bentley sitting in the back with a gun trained on him.

Fairlane sat down, water dripping from his clothing, and took the time to light a cigarette before saying anything.

"Mr. Fairlane?" Jack asked. Under his jacket, the 9mm was ready.

"Jim," Fairlane said. "Please call me Jim…I heard a lot about you from a previous customer, but I'll keep this brief; I want you to make a film for me."

"Is that so?" Jack asked. "What kind of film?"

"Let's not play games. You know what kind of film. I need girls, plenty of them, for a very particular client."

"Sure you do," Jack said. "Everyone wants it for someone else."

"Is that important to you?"

"Not at all, but what *is* important, Jim, is that if we are doing business together I need cash up front."

"That's fine," Fairlane said. "I'm willing to pay whatever you ask…within reason of course."

"There is no reasoning…just screaming," Jack said. "The standard price is $20,000, but how many girls are you talking about?"

"Four of them…" Jim said. "And I have the girls. They've already been paid…of course they don't know how it's going to end."

"Of course."

"And the client wants theatrics."

"What do you mean exactly?" Jack asked, pulling a cigarette case from his jacket.

"He wants them in garter belts, fishnets, and clown makeup."

Wow. There's a new one...and I thought the industry had lost its creativity.

"Why clowns?" Jack asked.

"Clowns and balloons...he wants plenty of balloons."

Jack hesitated, looked over at the Bentley and back to Jim.

"$100,000," Jack said, waiting for Fairlane to start laughing at the price, but he didn't.

"That's fine, John...but it better be good."

"Oh trust me," Jack said. "It'll be better than you can imagine."

Part III:
Perverse Therapy

Chapter Eight

From counseling to electroshock, the spectrum of therapy is nothing if not vast. Through hypnosis or psychotherapy the patient can delve into their buried past, stir up the root of whatever their problems are. Memories surface and so do answers; why they smoke, drink, fuck, cry, steal.

Maybe it was a lack of affection from their parents or maybe it was too much affection from a grabby uncle. Maybe they never find out why they do the things they do. Maybe, sometimes, it's better that way.

Therapy hadn't worked for Jack, and judging by the project requests that started coming in, he wasn't alone.

* * *

"When the phone rings with another client it means money, but it also means someone's been talking." Jack was once again imparting what he considered his infinite wisdom on Mikey as they drove back from Saint Michael's Parish.

"Not to mention this shit is really starting to get weird," was Mikey's only response.

"You're seriously going to start judging?"

"No, it's just...you know."

From the back of the recently-stolen utility van came a muffled cry, followed by a heavy thud against the rear sliding door.

"I guess he's awake."

"Guess so...are we seriously going through with this?"

"Yeah."

"Why?"

"$25,000 seems like a pretty good reason."

"Yeah, but this is fucked up even for you."

"What's the matter, you a lapse catholic with some leftover guilt or do you just have a soft spot for a man in uniform?"

"You know I'm in."

"I know this, but it's still fun to fuck with you," Jack said as he turned into the most recent hardware superstore to pop up along the highway. "Wait here and make sure he doesn't go anywhere."

"What if he starts praying?"

"Don't worry; his mouth is taped, so I don't think God will be able to hear him."

Mikey looked into the back, as Jack slammed the van door behind him. He saw the robes bloused out from beneath the nylon riot cuffs. The little beanie looking thing had rolled into the corner, and Father Bedard was now looking directly up at him, his eyes wide with fear.

"Jesus Christ," Mikey mumbled to himself before realizing the irony. "A fucking priest…"

Mikey turned back around, suddenly finding himself pulling at his collar and swallowing hard.

His phone vibrated.

"Pull the van around back; we got some wood to load up."

"Wood?" Mikey started, but the phone clicked off.

* * *

An hour later, Bedard and the supplies were in the basement, and Jack was down there with him. Mikey heard the sound of a nail gun as he unscrewed the cap from a bottle of Jim Beam took a long pull. He was coping with this one in his own way.

I'm gonna end up with whiskey dick…Hopefully I don't have to fuck this guy.

Downstairs the carpentry session finally ended and Jack trudged up and into the kitchen, wiping the sweat out of his hair and grabbing a beer from the refrigerator.

"Who says this isn't hard work?"

"What are bitching about? You're not the one that has to fuck a wrinkled old priest."

"Neither do you, shithead...well, not in the biblical sense anyhow." Jack smiled.

"Thank Christ."

"Well, I wouldn't go that far just yet."

"So what's the plan then?"

"Not a hundred percent on the script at the moment, but the set's done."

"I thought we already made our construction flick," Mikey took another swig of the whiskey, letting it burn down his throat and make his gut rumble. "What the fuck were you building down there anyway?"

"A cross."

"You're joking."

"Nope...not my idea of a good time, but I do what I'm paid for."

"And what were we paid for?"

"There's some creative leeway as far as the specifics are concerned, but this guy wants the priest to suffer. The crucifixion part was a must."

"I don't suppose he said why?"

"Apparently his childhood priest fucked him for years and his family never believed him. He lived with it for decades."

"And this is the priest?"

"No, he died last year, but it didn't seem to help erase the memories."

"So watching this is going to end it?"

"I don't know, maybe...not really my problem."

Mikey finished off the bottle and tossed it on top of the overflowing trashcan.

"Well, let's get this shit over with then."

* * *

The first nail went in with a small tear, between the thumb and forefinger of Father Bedard and into the solid oak of the makeshift cross he was tied to. It wasn't one of the three six-inch spikes waiting on the floor below him, but one from a container of two-inch box nails Jack had ceremoniously poured on his disrobed body after they started filming.

As prayer candles flickered in the background, Jack drove the second nail in between his index and middle fingers, another between the middle and ring. Mikey quietly did the same on the other hand.

Father Bedard wasn't as quiet, his screams nearly drowning out the Gregorian chants seeping in a monotone out of the stereo.

They continued down his arms and torso, every couple of inches pulling his wrinkled skin out from his body and forcing another nail through it. As Mikey worked between his toes, connecting his feet to the side of the cross, Jack pulled a long sterling silver crucifix out of his pocket. The spotlight shining down on Father Bedard's drooping head reflected off of it, causing a split-second glare in the lens of the camera. Jack rubbed the end of it against a knife sharpener until it created a crude point. Using the tip he started to dig it into Father Bedard's chest, writing:

Since you've acted like this, I won't stop until I get my revenge.

By the time he was done, Father Bedard had all but passed out and his blood had covered all of Judges 15:7 except for the word *revenge*.

"Time to wake him up," Jack shot Mikey a glance and picked up a bottle of vodka.

Father Bedard let out an almost inaudible moan.

"You want to bless this?" Jack laughed before throwing the liquor on him, jarring him awake and revealing his handy work.

Tears were rolling down his face and drool fell into the blood on Father Bedard's chest as Jack reached down and grabbed his balls.

"You ever betray a family's trust? Ever take out your repression by fucking a kid," Jack squeezed.

Father Bedard couldn't manage to form anything that resembled a word.

"Either way," Jack said, pulling the old man's cock out and pushing the three-inch base of the sharpened crucifix up his urethra.

Now he managed another scream, but quieted as he gave a little cough and blood dribbled from the corner of his mouth. Just as Father Bedard was about to lose consciousness again, Jack pushed him flat against the cross and snapped the crucifix in half, forcing a shard of silver out through the top of his cock.

Standing in the corner now, Mikey cringed at the sight and turned away, fighting back the bile tickling his throat.

"I need you over here," Jack said, picking the spikes and a mallet up off the floor of the basement.

He smashed one through Father Bedard's left wrist, the sound of bone crunching under the force as the spike pushed through his flesh and deep into the wood. The second spike did the same to his right wrist. The third went straight through his scrotum.

Each taking a side of the cross, Jack and Mikey lifted it and Father Bedard's diminished frame off the ground and leaned it against the exposed cinderblock wall of the basement.

Father Bedard's head hung loosely now. No sound coming from him except his bowels emptying, running down the blood-soaked wood and forming a puddle on the tarp they had stretched across the floor.

"Peace be with you," Jack whispered, switching the camera off.

Chapter Nine

Bill Corwin waited quietly at his desk in the upstairs office, browsing through last night's box scores before checking his online stock portfolio.

Sitting in his bathrobe with a cup of coffee, he could hear Marilyn downstairs in the kitchen running the blender, liquefying whatever the health concoction of the month was. Every day she drank that shit, went to the gym to see some $75-per-hour personal trainer and cooked from the pages of the newest fad diet books. Not that any of it did any good, her dumpy ass and sagging tits squeezed into matching track suits, the cottage cheese cellulite of her thighs bulging out a little more each day.

Downstairs the blender stopped.

"I'm heading out, honey," Marilyn's yell came up the stairs and down the hallway.

All those empty rooms—ever since Jenny left for college—provided plenty of distance between them.

"Okay," Bill muttered, still staring at the computer screen.

"What?"

"I said 'okay'."

Jenny, though—sorry, she went by Jennifer now—was still the name on the credit card and tuition bills rolling in every month, five years after she started "studying" performance arts.

Jenny was Bill and Marilyn's eldest now, but she wasn't their first.

In college, Marilyn hadn't been that different from Jenny, not exactly promiscuous but no saint. Mistakes happen, condoms break, and periods are missed. Like mother like daughter, but abortion wasn't an option for Marilyn.

She cried when the newborn was turned over to the adoption agency and post partum depression set in. In the end, she never finished school, the reason she decided not to keep the boy in the first place. And when Jenny came along five years later, Marilyn dedicated every waking moment to pampering her. She spoiled her right up through high school, bending her and Bill's lives to Jenny's every whim.

When Jenny left for college, Marilyn fell into depression again. For two years she ate everything she could fit in her grubby little mouth. For the next two years she exercised and had regular colonics. The cellulite turned into stretch marks, which were later complimented with cosmetic surgery scars. Whatever the phase, whatever the craze, it never came cheap.

Like mother like daughter.

"Alright, I'm off. I love you," Marilyn's shout snapped Bill back to reality.

"Uh huh...you too."

Bill had an hour before he would leave for the office. He listened for the garage door, Marilyn's SUV backing out of the driveway, the door going back down again. Peering from between the blinds he watched as the rear end of her Explorer disappeared around the corner. He minimized the browser window, brought up a new window and typed in the address of a porn trade website.

In the past few years this had become a morning ritual. It was the only time it was truly quiet—save the occasional fake moan coming from the computer speakers. It was also the only time Bill could forget about the bills, mundane office routine, his receding hairline, cellulite stretched track suits, high fiber diets, prostate checks, and Jenny...*fucking Jenny.*

Bill clicked through the video category list.

Abused, Adorable, Amateur...Farm, Femdom, Fisting...Midget, MILF, Military...Rectal Examine, Redhead, Rim Job...Water Sports, Webcam, Wired Pussy.

The Rectal Examine link conjured up images of Bill's last physical, but worse than that, he was tired of all this. What started with centerfolds turned into straight porn turned into anal and bondage. Now, if some pock-marked bitch with daddy issues and her roots showing wasn't screaming as a wiffle ball bat was shoved up her ass, he had a hard time getting off.

Every morning he managed, though.

* * *

A quick shower and long commute later, Bill was sitting in his windowless office, staring at a blank computer screen while his supervisor Ted was bitching through the intercom system of his phone.

Progress reports…board of directors waiting…downsizing…

This was another morning ritual, though admittedly not as fun. Bill had been with the company for going on twelve years now, but he still wasn't surely exactly what to tell people when they asked him what he did for a living. His business cards read "William Corwin, Regional Director of Information and Marketing," but in the last three years the only place in that region he'd ventured was this same dingy, cramped office.

"Are you even listening," Ted's voice boomed through the intercom.

Shut the fuck up you pompous douche bag.

"Uh huh," Bill mumbled back.

"Then get on it."

I hope you get cancer.

"Yes, sir."

Bill clicked the phone off and stared at the monitor for a few more minutes. Someone else would eventually do whatever the hell Ted was on about this morning, and come time for his annual evaluation, Bill would take the credit. In the meantime, he busied himself with computer solitaire.

* * *

Sometime around 10 a.m., Steve popped his head into Bill's office for their daily bullshit session, a coffee break that usually lasted the better part of an hour and a half. Who needed a real therapist when you could just bitch about your wife and kids to someone who hated his almost as much? A licensed therapist, on the other hand, probably wouldn't have fucked your daughter three days after her 18th birthday like Steve had.

Fucking Jenny.

"What's going on?" Steve plopped himself down in the worn chair sitting in front of Bill's cluttered desk.

"Eh, same old shit."

"Yeah."

The two of them sat in silence for a few minutes, forced to think about how, well into middle age, this was the highlight of their social interaction. Time had run out for a fresh start years ago, and this was as good as it was going to get. Life had won and the only thing left to do was make the best of it.

"What do you say we get the fuck out of here?" Steve interjected, just as the silence was officially becoming awkward. "We can grab a drink. Plus I've got something to show you."

"I've seen it before. I wasn't all that impressed."

"Just shut up and call Teddy boy."

"I am. Hold on," Bill dialed Ted's intercom number. "Ted, Bill Corwin here, I forgot to tell you earlier about the client lunch scheduled for noon. I'll probably be gone most of the afternoon, if not the whole day."

"Did you at least finish the progress reports for the board?"

"Sure did," Bill lied.

"Alright, we'll go over it tomorrow."

"Absolutely," Bill hung up, turning to Steve. "Let's get the fuck out of here before he decides to come along."

* * *

They were barely in the door before Steve was behind the wood-stained bar in the corner of the basement rec room. Pouring three fingers of Macallan into two glasses, he was over to the couch before Bill even got his tie loosened.

"You've got to see this," he said, flipping on the plasma TV mounted to the wall in front of them.

"What is it?"

"You'll see." Steve pressed play on the DVD player and the screen went black for a few seconds before the face of a forty-something woman's mascara and tear-streaked face filled the frame, a barbed-wire ball gag cutting into the laugh lines at the corner of her mouth. She was pulled back by the hair as the masked man behind her yanked up on her cuffed hands, popping her shoulders out of the sockets. She screamed, but all that came out was a muffled protest, more tears and a trickle of blood than ran down her chin.

"That looks just like…" Bill started.

"Samantha, I know. It's fucking great isn't it?"

"It's not actually her, though…?"

"Of course not, imagine how fast they'd trace that one back to me."

Mikey pushed the Samantha lookalike to a tarp-covered floor and latched her hands above her head to a grappling hook coming out the cement wall. He spread her legs and put her feet through cinder blocks at the bottom of the tarp. Sitting on top of her, he pulled out an industrial stapler.

"So, who is it then?"

"I don't know, some random whore. I just described what I wanted and they got the bitch," Steve said.

"Who did?"

"The producers, two guys, one of them said his name was John or something."

Mikey reached off camera, bringing back a stack of dollar bills. One-by-one he put bills on the woman's back and pumped carpet staples through them. Her blood soaked through the money as Mikey worked his way down her ass and legs with the stapler.

"How did you meet these guys," Bill tried to hide his hard-on with a throw pillow.

"Friend of a client."

"They do good work."

When he finished covering her back, Mikey wiped his hand through her blood and used it to cover his cock before pushing it into her ass. He fucked her for what seemed like a full 15 minutes before pulling out of her, bringing with him a trail of come. Putting the remaining bills against her snatch, Mikey used a hunting knife to make sure they went all the way in. She let out a whimper, the knife handle still jutting from between her legs. Mikey took her by the hair again and started slamming her face against the floor. Somewhere around the time her nose snapped for the fourth time, she let out her last whimper.

"Pretty fucking impressive, huh?" Steve asked.

"I just can't get over how much she looks like Samantha."

"I'm considering it a lump sum payment for some good therapy, after all the money that bitch took when she left—an anti-alimony treatment if you will."

"Does it work?"

"Two or three times a day since I got it," Steve laughed.

* * *

Bill's cell phone rang while he was driving home, reliving what he'd watched that afternoon. He took it out of his pocket and looked at the caller ID on the front: JENNY.

"Hey honey, how's school?"

"It's alright, dad. Hey, listen, I can't really talk right now, but I needed to ask you a favor."

"Uh huh."

"I need money."

"Jenny, I just sent you a check last week."

"Yeah, but that was for books. I need cash to get my teeth whitened. My acting coach said it could make the difference between landing a real acting job and being stuck doing community theatre. Oh, and how many times to do I have to tell you I go by Jennifer now?"

"Sorry, I forgot. How much do you need?"

"At least $800."

"For your fucking teeth? I swear, between you and your mother…"

"She already said it was fine."

"Of course she did."

"So you can send it tomorrow then?"

"Do I have a choice?"

Jennifer ignored the question.

"Thanks, daddy. Love you. Gotta go," she hung up.

Bill closed his phone and turned up the radio as the freeway traffic in front of him slowed down to a crawl. He drummed on the steering wheel with his thumbs for awhile and wished he still smoked. Finally, the Regional Director of Information and Marketing opened his phone back up and hit one of the speed dial numbers.

It rang five times on the other before an obviously out-of-breath Steve answered.

"What are you doing?" Bill asked.

"What the fuck do you think," Steve's laugh boomed through the receiver.

"Never mind. Hey, do you think I can get that John guy's number?"

Chapter Ten

Since the cash started rolling in Jack had almost forgotten his vanity, but with a lapse between projects, it came flooding back. He had bursts of anger toward Mikey for the way he lived, the way he dressed. A fucking slob with no self-respect.

And worse than that he wasn't getting any credit. Mikey was the star and the police were too fucking stupid to figure anything out yet. Hell, even the victims became immortalized, something to be jerked off to for generations to come, no pun intended.

Every few nights on the news there were reports of another missing girl, an update on the last girl, a priest who never showed up for mass. It was always "tragic" or "mysterious." Family members cried in front of the cameras, pleading for someone to call them, their precious daughter or niece or wife would never just up and leave. But in the end, no one ever made the connection and the program moved on to discuss the best way to lose weight with vinegar or how to know if canned vegetables could give you breast cancer.

"The whole thing is fucking sad," Jack said no one in particular as he stared into the mirror, considering whether or not his eyebrows were too far apart.

"What's the plan?" Mikey popped his head in the door.

"For what?"

"For today, what are we doing?"

"Going to find you a co-star," Jack shot back. "And put a clean fucking shirt on."

* * *

In the past few months, Mikey had seen a lot, but this guy was something different. He wanted a girl who looked like his daughter. She was supposed to be a college student, brunette, brown eyes. He even gave them her measurements. They were supposed to call her Jenny on screen. She should be wearing a University of the Arts t-shirt. The guy knew what he wanted, but it bothered Mikey. The whole thing reminded him of his family; his sister, their dad, and the shit he had seen growing up.

Before Heather, he had never killed anyone, but now that he'd gotten through it, Mikey wished he had started with his father.

Mike took his share of the abuse, filling in as a punching bag when his dad came home drunk and angry. His little sister, Tara, suffered the brunt of it, though, becoming the focus when he came home drunk and horny. Mikey tried to intervene but that just delayed it for a few minutes until the beating was over. Tara bled on a regular basis long before she ever got her period.

Mikey left home when Tara was 15. It was the night after their dad showed a spark of creativity and broke out the camcorder, forcing the two of them to fuck on camera while a couple of his hunting buddies watched.

After that, Mikey ran; stealing, squatting, and getting high until he ended up in California. Six months later, a friend from back home gave him the news. Without Mikey around, Tara got all the attention, and one night dad went too far and fractured her skull. Tara had died in the hospital early the next morning. She was six-months pregnant.

Despite all he'd seen and done since going along with Jack's plans, his sister's was the only death Mikey couldn't forgive himself for. The rest were just nameless faces and pussies, but this latest order struck a nerve.

"Let's get going," Jack called from the hallway.

Unfortunately, Mikey hadn't learned to say no to Jack yet.

* * *

Mikey remembered the look on Tara's face when he was on top of her, as he and Jack circled the University of the Arts campus on the south side of town looking for a girl who met the description.

Both of them were crying, Mikey whispering "I'm sorry" over and over again as their dad and his friends laughed from behind the camera.

It was a Friday evening, and the campus was relatively empty as Mikey continued to steer the van in circles, looping around the dorms, classrooms, and athletic fields a few times before cutting away from the campus to divert any attention.

The third or fourth time around, Jack spotted a girl leaving the theatre alone and pointed her out to Mikey. They trailed her from a distance, Jack with binoculars pressed up against his face.

At seventeen, Mikey had been something of a recluse and never managed to go out and get laid like the rest of his classmates. Tara was his first time. It was also the last time he spoke to her. Leaving late that night, the last words he said to his little sister were "I'm sorry."

"I can't tell if she'll do," Jack said, letting the binoculars drop into his lap. "She's the right height and build, but I can't make out her eye color."

"Does it really matter? This guy isn't going to be looking at her eyes."

"He was very specific, specific enough to toss in an extra $5,000 to make sure the details were right. So we're going to make sure the details are right."

"Fine, let's just get this over with."

"What's wrong with you?"

Mikey didn't answer, just slowly followed the girl as she walked off campus and headed down the street, stopping in at a pizza shop.

"Pull over here," Jack said, already out the door.

Jack disappeared into the pizzeria, a few paces behind the girl, and Mikey waited for what seemed like hours.

And he was sorry. Sorry for that night. Sorry for all the nights before it when he was helpless to stop him.

The click of the rear van door snapped Mikey out of his daze, and he wiped his eyes before Jack popped his head up front.

"You want to toss me that duct tape and maybe think about getting the fuck out of here?" Jack asked.

In the back of the van, the girl was screaming and biting at Jack's hand. An elbow to the side of her face slowed her down enough to tape her mouth shut, though, and Jack worked his way down, taping her hands and feet. He gave her one more shot to the back of the head, putting her out, before making his way back up to the passenger's seat.

"That was easy enough," he smiled. "Bitch is already wearing the right shirt too. There's $20 saved."

Mikey stared at him, his eyes vacant like they were that last night at home. Jack was still prattling on beside him, but he was unable to focus on what he was saying, something about industry, therapy and all the good they were doing. None of it mattered. All his bullshit aside, Jack was in it for the money, and that was fine; Mikey had finally come to terms with what they were doing.

"Are you even listening to me?" Jack asked.

"Huh? Yeah…extreme therapy, saving the world, all that shit, right?"

"Yes, but it's not that simple," Jack raised his voice to be heard over the van's engine and the girl's cries.

"You know you're full of shit, right?"

Jack was looking at himself in the vanity mirror on the back of the sun visor.

"That bitch scratched me," he said, touching a small trickle of blood on his left cheek.

"You're not even listening are you?"

"What? Yeah, sure I am."

"Whatever." Mikey drove the rest of the way in silence.

* * *

By the time the girl woke up, she was already in the basement, duct taped to a chair, wearing nothing but the University of the Arts t-shirt. It was dark and took her eyes a minute to adjust. When they did, she realized she was alone. The room was quiet, still. She listened carefully but didn't hear anyone upstairs either.

She jerked her body forward, moving the chair with her. She didn't see a phone, and tried to inch her way toward the stairs, throwing all her weight against the tape that was digging into her ankles, thighs and wrists.

Heaving, breathless, she finally made it to the bottom of the stairs, tipping over in the chair and starting to push herself up using her feet and elbows. Those dance classes were paying off already.

She was about halfway up when she heard it, the front door slamming shut and what sounded like two men in a heated conversation. Stuck in the middle, she froze, silently sobbing as the footsteps approached the door above her.

"I don't know why the fuck you can't just drop it," one of the voices said.

"Because it's important you understand why we're doing this."

"Oh, I understand…it's called money."

"No…well, yes…but that's not all it's about."

"That's right you're the fucking amateur psychiatrist over here…"

The knob at the top of the stairs turned.

"I'm just saying it's not as one-sided as you make it out to be. Who are we to decide what people need to overcome past trauma."

"Just admit that it's about the…"

"Oh, what the fuck?" Jack was looking down the stairs at the newest client's fantasy. "Exactly where do you think you're going sweetheart?"

She looked up at him, tears in her bloodshot eyes, snot drying on the ball gag and rug burn all over her elbows. She screamed, but it got trapped behind the hard plastic of the gag. Jack frowned, planted a boot against her neck and kicked her back down to the bottom of the stairs.

"That's better."

"Jack," Mikey called from behind him but got no response.

"Jack!"

"What?" Jack barked back without turning around.

"I'm fairly certain the guy who contracted this is going to want her alive…at least until we kill her."

Now, Jack turned around and looked up at Mikey.

"Sorry, I got a bit anxious." Jack laughed for the first time in quite a while.

* * *

When she woke up in the basement for the second time, it was much lighter, bright in fact. She squinted against what seemed like spotlights, with two silhouetted figures moving around behind the blinding white spots. Her head throbbed, the iron taste of blood in her mouth. Running her cracked tongue around the inside of her mouth she realized she was missing at least three teeth. The ballgag was gone.

She tried to spit, but her mouth was dry and all that came out was a long croak.

"Look who's awake," Jack called across the room to Mikey, who was busy ghosting the hard drive of any evidence.

"It's about time," Mikey said. "There's a *Muppets* special on tonight I want to watch. So let's get this done."

"What?"

"*The Muppets Go Hollywood*...oh, never mind, just get her ready, would you?"

"I liked this better when I was running everything," Jack shot back, walking over to the girl, who now looked as equally confused as she was scared.

"So you're a student, huh?" Jack asked, taking a wet rag and wiping the dried blood from the side of the girl's face and pushing her hair back out of her eyes. All he got back was a teary-eyed gaze.

"Fine, I was just trying to make conversation," he tossed the rag into the corner behind a camera the girl had just noticed.

Walking over to the camera, Jack adjusted the focus, fidgeting with the zoom and then moving around the set with a light meter Not that they'd ever received any complaints, but *if you're going to do a thing do it right.*

"Yes," came the whisper.

"What was that?" Jack turned back toward the girl.

"I'm a student."

"And what do you study?"

"Acting."

"Well that's perfect," Jack said, "because we're about to give you your big break."

"What are you going to do to me?"

"Make you a star."

"How..." she stammered. "What the fuck does that mean?"

Jack reached in his back pocket and pulled out a pair of gripping pliers. By now, Mikey was behind the camera and Jack was pulling a mask over his face as the record light flashed red.

"You'll figure it out soon enough." Jack smiled as he pulled the girl's head back by her hair. "Now open wide."

The way she screamed, Jack wished he could keep the gag in while he did this. Four of her teeth were already gone from the face plant she took on the bottom step of the stairs, but there were still 28 to go, and this cunt wasn't about to stop screaming.

"Would you please shut the fuck up?" Jack spoke calmly. "I'm trying to work here."

She spat blood on him.

The orthodontistry thing had something do with the client's daughter. He was pissed at her for all the money she cost, starting with braces at age 10. Now, he said, she was still sucking him dry, wasting her time and his retirement plans on art school. He had described her in detail. This was his therapy. Reversing the spending. Treating himself. Having done to this girl what he could never do to his own daughter.

Somewhere around the lateral incisor the girl passed out, her blood now soaking through the University of the Arts t-shirt she still had on.

Mikey kept the shot tight on her mouth. The client had been very specific. He wanted to watch everything close up. Jack shoved a finger in the hole where her second molar had been and the girl jolted awake with the strangest noise he'd ever heard a human make, something like a moan that had been regurgitated all the way up from her diaphragm. He looked in her eyes, seeing a certain deadness, as he finished with her teeth. Then he moved on to her tongue, using kitchen scissors to make short work of removing it.

If his daughter is anything like this girl I'd want her to shut up too.

His cock did the trick, as he forced it into her toothless mouth, past where her tongue had been just a minute ago and felt her tonsils. She threw up then, the blood and bile making his public hair wet and sticky. He stopped just before he was about to come.

From there, Jack moved on to her fingernails, using a paring chisel to pry them off one at a time.

Daddy didn't like paying for all those manicures.

The toenails went next. Then he used a pair of gardening shears to take off two of her fingers. Close up after close up. He used her recently removed digits to finger her pussy. Then he switched to a wire coat hanger.

You thought he didn't know about the abortion, huh? Maybe you shouldn't have used a credit card. Another $600 wasted, sweetheart.

Finally, Mikey zoomed out, framing the shot as Jack fucked the pulpy mess of what used to be her pussy. It was so loose by then that he had to finish in her ass, though. She would have died on her own in a few hours, or maybe minutes, but for good measure, he wanted to finish it on camera.

The shot focused on her face as Jack put a hunting knife in her mouth and leaned his weight down on it until she stopped choking. The last shot was of a pool of blood forming between her tits, the tip of the knife coming out from inside her throat and creating a glare on the "A" in Arts.

Chapter Eleven

Back at home, Bill Corwin was anxious, excited. He'd paid for the film more than a week ago and was still waiting for the phone call that it was done. In the meantime, he'd had a change of heart where his wife was concerned.

The prospect of something altogether new was arousing, almost to the point of intoxicating, and his disposition had changed for the better. Marilyn had noticed. They ate dinner together for the first time in months, didn't argue about money all week, and were even talking about taking a weekend getaway when her yoga class ended. Bill had also stopped jerking off every morning.

He was a changed man before his private therapy session even started. Now all he had to do was wait.

* * *

His cell phone rang that afternoon as he sat in his office, working on the crossword puzzle in the morning paper. Monday's puzzle he had a shot at, but by Friday, he was fucked and realized just how little he really knew.

The number came up "Unknown," and Bill wonder who was calling for a few seconds before it dawned on him and his heart skipped a beat. Taking a breath he flipped open the phone.

"This is Bill."

"Bill, it's John."

"How are you?"

"It's ready." Jack skipped the small talk.

"Great. How does this work?"

"You're going to meet me in 45 minutes beneath the overpass at Exit 141…bring the other half of the money."

"I'm at work right now."

"Forty-five minutes."

"Okay. Okay. I'll be there."

The phone went dead, and Bill hung up, taking another breath and trying to compose himself before pushing the intercom button and dialing Ted's extension.

"Ted, I'm feeling a little under the weather. I think I'm going to take a few hours of sick time this afternoon," he tried to hide his excitement as he spoke.

"Are the progress reports done?"

"Yes, sir."

Bill still had no idea which reports he was talking about. He was too busy thinking about what was waiting for him under the overpass.

"Okay then. I'll see you tomorrow." Ted hung up.

Bill was down to the parking garage in record time, first checking, then double checking, that the rest of the cash was in his trunk, and then taking off out of the garage and squealing onto the street.

It took ten minutes to get to Exit 141; he still had half an hour and pulled into a gas station beside the on-ramp. Bill hadn't smoked in almost a decade, but he walked inside and asked for a pack of Parliaments. He hadn't been this excited since he lost his virginity to his second cousin, Emily, after the town Christmas parade more than 30 years ago. He needed a cigarette, and all things considered, it was the least of his vices at the moment.

As he merged onto the highway, Bill had half a hard-on, pictures of Emily and Jenny and the tape Steve had shown him flashing in his imagination. He started to rub his cock through his pants and barely noticed when he almost drifted out of his lane and into the side of a tractor trailer. The driver pulled his horn, snapping Bill back to reality for a few seconds. He righted the car and tried to focus on driving, but it had been a week since he last got off, and he struggled to concentrate as the lap of his Dockers khakis bulged.

Just when he thought he couldn't take it anymore, Bill saw the sign. "Exit 141 – ¼ mile."

He merged right, exited, and swung the car under the overpass, killing the engine. Bill was alone for the moment, craning his neck to look for another car. When he turned back around someone knocked on the passenger's side window, making him jump out of his seat. It was someone he hadn't seen before, and Bill just cracked the window.

"Who the fuck are you?"

"Jeff," Mikey answered.

"Where is John?"

"He sent me."

"Why the hell should I believe you?"

"Because if you don't, you don't get this." Mikey tapped an unmarked DVD case on the window.

Bill hesitated for a minute before reaching over and unlocking the door. Mikey got inside, sat down and pointed toward the pack of Parliaments sitting on the dashboard.

"Think I can get one of those?"

"Sure." Bill took two cigarettes out of the pack and handed one to Mikey. "So can I have the DVD now?"

"Money first." Mikey lit the cigarette.

"You sure sound like John."

"Common interests. Where's the cash?"

Bill went to the trunk and came back with the kind of dufflebag they give away at minor league baseball games. He threw it on Mikey's lap.

"Classy," Mikey said, looking down at the bag.
"I didn't know you were so picky or I would've put it in Prada," Bill said, finally getting his confidence back.

Mikey laughed and unzipped the bag, thumbing through bundles of twenties.

"Good enough," he tossed the DVD on Bill's backseat, opened the door and started to get out.

"That's it?" Bill asked.

"That's it. Enjoy."

And with that Mikey was gone, already half a dozen paces behind the car and not slowing down. Bill reached behind his seat and picked up the DVD He stared at the black plastic case for a few seconds, then opened it up to find a burned disc that simply read "therapy session no. 1" in black permanent marker.

Jack had a less-than-ordinary sense of humor.

Closing the case, Bill put it in his glove box, started the car, and headed back toward the highway.

* * *

Fuck.

When Bill pulled into his driveway, he saw his wife's SUV parked in the garage. He hoped she'd be out. All he could think about was the DVD sitting in his glove box. He wanted to watch it. He needed to watch it. He needed it fucking now.

But Marilyn was home and obviously in for the evening, already in sweats and lying on the couch when he went inside.

"How was your day," she mumbled, more interested in the primetime game show flashing in front of her than his response.

"Uneventful. How was yours?"

"Eh."

"I'm going to order a pizza. You hungry?"

"What?...No...I already ate."

An hour later Bill sat at the kitchen table beside a half eaten pizza, trying—to no avail—to read the evening paper. The Business and Sports sections were spread out in front of him, but all he could think about was come and blood, pussy, and pain.

Marilyn waddled into the kitchen.

"I'm going to bed," she announced.

"Okay, good night."

"I'm leaving early tomorrow, I have to go to the gym early so I can meet Brenda for breakfast."

"Okay."

I finally catch a break around here.

Bill heard Marilyn upstairs, banging around the bathroom in her nighttime ritual; washing her face, brushing her teeth, and doing whatever the fuck else she did in there. He thought about going to bed himself but knew he wouldn't be getting much sleep that night. He finally fell asleep at three a.m., watching sports highlights on TV.

* * *

Bill dialed his office number quickly.

Marilyn had woken him on her way out five minutes earlier. The sun was still coming up through the kitchen window as he waited for the automated, before-hours message to pick up. Once it did, he punched in Ted's extension number and waited for his voicemail.

"Ted, Bill Corwin here," he said with his best fake cold. "I'm not feeling much better than yesterday afternoon. So, I don't think I'm going to make it in today. Anything you need, just give Steve a buzz, and hopefully I'll see you tomorrow."

Bill hung up. One obstacle down. He put on a pot of coffee as he waited to make sure Marilyn wouldn't come back for anything. When he was sure she gone for the morning, he walked out to the garage, retrieving the DVD and cigarettes from his car.

He grabbed a cup of coffee and headed upstairs to the home office. Flipping on the computer, he set a box of tissues and the coffee on the desk. He lit a cigarette and waited for the start-up menus and security updates to finish before putting the DVD in the computer tray.

He wanted everything to be perfect, but he needed to slow down. His cock was already pushing its way through the folds of the bathrobe he was wearing.

Forcing himself to finish the cigarette before opening the desktop media player, he took a sip of coffee and finally hit PLAY.

There were no titles. No credits. No fucking around. The picture on his screen went from black straight to a close up of a girl's mouth, pliers inside pulling her teeth one by one. She screamed. It was exactly what he had asked for, but somehow he still couldn't believe what he was seeing.

They did it. They actually fucking did it. There's no way that's fake.

Bill was already stroking his cock, without even fully realizing it, and the next thing he knew he was about to come. Grabbing a handful of tissues, he held out until he saw Jack's cock going into the girl's mouth. Then he lost it, missing the tissues almost completely and drenching the keyboard with a week's worth of backed up jizz.

He clicked pause.

He had all morning, and for $30,000, he was going to enjoy every minute of this.

Bill cleaned up the keyboard, washed his hands and lit another cigarette. He drank his coffee and went online, scrolling through the news briefs that popped up on his homepage.

He tried to forget about the DVD for a few minutes, but couldn't get what he'd just seen out of his mind. And before he knew it, Bill was getting hard again. It had only been half an hour or so, and he couldn't believe it. He hadn't been like this since he was nineteen. Once a day had been more than enough since about two years after he married Marilyn.

You can't argue with science, though.

Bill stubbed out what was now his fifth cigarette of the morning and clicked PLAY again, the video on the screen picking up from where he had left off. The images flickered in front of him.

Fingernails being pried off...

That'll teach that bitch.

Being violated with her own chopped off fingers...

Fucking Jenny.

A coat hanger destroying her twat...

Jenny, you soiled fucking cunt.

Getting fucked in the wound...

Fucking Jenny.

By now, Bill was going full steam. Cock in hand, he was jerking furiously, the images on screen mixing with the face of his daughter. He was building up to climax again.

The camera shot started to pull out, showing the girl's blood stained tits in her t-shirt. The man on screen had a knife now. He was getting ready to kill her, and just as he pushed the knife down and the shot widened to show the girl's face, Bill came again.

And there it was. That face. The face of his daughter. Only this time it was on the screen.

* * *

Fucking Jenny was the last thought Bill had before he saw the tip of the knife come jutting out from inside her throat.

Then he collapsed back into the desk chair, his hand and leg covered with come. In shock, he couldn't move, couldn't stop the video. Sitting there on a Wednesday morning, all he could do was watch as his daughter died in front of him.

The screen went black.

Chapter Twelve

A few hours later, Bill was still trying to recover.

He'd paced around the house for what seemed like days, drinking the better part of a bottle of Irish whiskey he found in the liquor cabinet. The alcohol hadn't helped. Nothing had helped; not the booze or the shower or trying to think about something else, anything else.

Bill had seen his daughter die. He had paid for it and he had got off to it. Twice.

How could this happen? How the fuck could this happen? How could it have been her. It couldn't have been her.

But it had been her.

Fucking Jenny.

He hadn't meant for it to happen, but it had. There was no going back.

Sure, I described her well, but what are the fucking chances? I said a University of the Arts t-shirt, but I didn't think they'd actually go to the school, just order a shirt. What the fuck was I thinking?

Bill continued to pace around his home office, but he couldn't get away from the guilt that was building, as a clear picture of what he had done finally came into focus. He needed to get out of the house.

The best he could hope for was to turn the guilt into blame, and he did his best as he got into his car and took off down the street.

He wasn't sure where he was going, but it had to be better than here.

* * *

The sun came up through the windshield of Bill's car early the next morning, bringing with it the worst day of his life and a fairly severe hangover.

A minute or two passed before Bill realized where he was and why. Parked under the Exit 141 overpass, it all came flooding back; the video, Jenny, her blood, his come, the cash.

He wanted to be anyone else right then. He wished it was him instead of Jenny, but it wasn't, and he had no choice but to go home and try and figure it all out.

When Bill got home Marilyn's car was back in the garage, but when he went inside it was empty, quiet. He absentmindedly opened the refrigerator and looked inside. Nothing. He wasn't hungry. It was just force of habit. He went upstairs and sat on the bed, exhausted...drained.

Bill nodded off for an hour, his nightmares full of scenes from what he had seen yesterday.

When he woke, Bill went back down to the kitchen. He checked the garage. Marilyn's car was still there, but he hadn't heard anything from her since he'd been home. Maybe she'd caught a ride to the gym with Brenda.

It was then Bill made a decision. He was going to clean himself up, destroy the DVD, and try to move past this. He'd never forgive himself for what he'd done, but he wasn't going to bring Marilyn into it. She'd loved him unconditionally, stuck with him through everything, and he wasn't going to let it ruin her life. They'd made it through the adoption together, and they'd make it through this too.

First things first, though. He had to get rid of the evidence, destroy the disc and put it behind him.

Upstairs in his office, Bill sat down to turn the computer on, but when he touched the mouse, the screen came to life. In his haste yesterday he must not have turned it off. On the screen was the black video viewer of the media player. Minimized below it was an Internet browser window that read "Delicious Diet Recipes." Marilyn had been on the computer.

Panic hit him.

What if she saw...please don't let her have seen it...

Bill felt himself wretch, the thought of his wife seeing the video bringing up the sting of the whiskey from last night. He made a straight line for the bathroom, trying to hold back the vomit, but when reached the doorway, Bill froze.

There was Marilyn, soaking in the bathtub, her wrist split open from the elbow to the palm of her hand.

The water was blood red.

Marilyn was paler than he'd ever seen her.

Beside the tub lay his grandfather's antique straight-edge razor, the one they kept on display on the small glass shelf above the toilet.

Bill couldn't hold the rotten contents of his stomach in any longer.

* * *

Marilyn Sanders had been up and off to the gym early that morning. She hadn't even noticed her husband's absence on her rush out the door.

It was a typical day in what her life had become. A training session, a decaf skim latte, and some shopping before coming home and looking for ways to pass the afternoon.

Following the second half of a soap opera she had made her way upstairs and was searching for recipes involving pomegranates—her newest kick in a long line of antioxidants. The computer had seemed bogged down as she browsed the concoctions online, and she noticed a DVD-ROM icon spinning in the bottom right corner of the desktop screen. Curious, Marilyn had played the disc her husband had left resting in the computer.

She knew what Bill did up here after she left in the morning. The spent tissues and shady credit card charges made it obvious, but what she saw that morning was beyond anything her imagination could have whipped up. Porno, sure. She even tweaked her libido now and again with some adult entertainment, but what was on that DVD was something else entirely.

Try as she might, though, Marilyn had let her morbid curiosity get the best of her and made it through the DVD—only turning away at a few of the particularly horrendous scenes. Then, almost twenty minutes into the film, there it was: Jenny's face. Her daughter's face on screen, twisted in agony, toothless and bleeding.

That's when Marilyn Sanders had lost it.

Burning pomegranate juice had pushed its way up past her esophagus and tears streamed down her cheeks. Her daughter. Her only fucking daughter and this had happened. And why did Bill have this?

As she paced around the house trying to come to terms with what she had seen. There was no call, no demands, just her rape and death captured in every gruesome detail.

Marilyn drew a bath. She needed to relax her shaking body; she needed time to figure all this out. The last time emotion had overwhelmed her like this was during her pregnancy in college. Bill had convinced her to give the boy up for adoption, and Marilyn suffered from postpartum depression for months following the birth. When Jenny was born, she had managed to push the adoption out of her mind—instead focusing on pampering her baby daughter.

Bill had been less than thrilled at the way she treated Jenny, and as she grew older—and spent more of his money—it had only gotten worse. Bill had always been...

Bill. The answer hit Marilyn in the gut as she eased herself into the tub. This was no accident, no kidnapping, no coincidence. This had something to do with Bill and his vaguely masked hatred for their daughter.

It had been all Marilyn could take to watch her daughter die, but with this new realization piled on top, all reason slipped away. She scrambled out of the tub and grabbed the antique straight-razor. Before she'd let her husband's true perversions invade her imagination, Marilyn had ended it—thoughts of Jenny, the adoption, and her husband's evil spiraling toward the bathtub drain alongside the blood from her wrist.

Part IV:
The Circus is Coming

Chapter Thirteen

Jack Sanders was dreaming, Mikey on the floor beside him, his wife beater covered in Cheetos, blood, and beer.

Dead asleep, Jack was at the circus, watching the ferris wheel turn as he stood among the crowds. It was the one week every fall the traveling show invaded the small, Podunk town he grew up in. The week always ended on Halloween.

Jack turned in his sleep, his eyes moving calmly beneath their lids. His thoughts rushed like a movie stuck in fast forward, and he was home now. The smell of his foster mother's roses on the table and her god-awful perfume creating a less-then appealing ambiance, like a cloud of torturous marsh gas. He was in his childhood room now, door closed. Sophomore year, his best days still ahead.

Jack dabbed on the last touches of make-up. He leaned back in his chair and took a long look at himself in the mirror. Very theatrical. His skin was as white as a lunar surface—and only a little less cratered—his lipstick thick and harlot red. Deep blue, the color of nightshades surrounded his eyes, his nose claret. He was a clown, and they would all die laughing.

To them he was nothing, but that was fine by him. He didn't fit in and would make that apparent with every bullet. He noticed a small patch of pink under his jaw, picked up his powder brush, and went to work. Some people might think it was a nuisance to get up and do this every day, but it pacified him...usually. His parents didn't like him being different, although at the time, mom was very different. And they didn't understand why he liked it that way. His foster mother said it was the reason he didn't have friends, although she would've never guessed it. She said it was a form of self-hatred, a deliberate attempt to become an outcast. He laughed and told her she didn't make a very good psychologist. He told her the same thing at her funeral. His dad said it was just punk fashion, all 15-year-old boys needed to experiment, and by next year, he'd be normal again. But Jack wasn't a punk and rolled his eyes at his dad's dated notions of youth sub-culture. There was nothing interesting or attractive about giving up individuality to follow crowds, and after all, this was Halloween, the one time a year it was okay to be different. One day out of the year it was socially acceptable to wear a mask and be somebody else for a change.

At school they reviled him. He didn't kid himself about that; he was an outsider, but he knew underneath it all there was more to it. The occult held an air of mystery and an element of fear. Even the biggest, toughest, most popular guys in school avoided him, and deep down, it was because of fear. To hold that kind of power over those kind of guys gave Jack Sanders a kick. In the make-up he felt powerful.

Jack finished brushing powder on his face and looked in the mirror again. His reflection stared back at him like a cartoon mime dead in a crypt. He ran a hand through his hair and let a few limp black strands fall down his face and in front of his eyes. With a little chuckle, he grinned, bared his teeth, picked up the gun from his desk, and headed out.

The Volkswagen pulled up beside the gym, fifty yards from the main gate of the basketball courts. Jack thanked his mom for the ride and reminded himself he'd kill her later. All the shit she did to him, what did she expect?

Jack took his backpack from beside him and stepped out onto the sidewalk and into the crisp autumn air. Through the metal railings he could see the parking lot, an excited, swarming, noisy chaos, too exuberant for the time of morning.

When he walked through the gates, a short, stocky boy hopped off the wall in front of the teacher's parking lot and strolled up to him. It was true Jack had no friends, but he and Toby had been put on an assignment together—the only two left without partners—and had struck up an odd kinship. Toby was smart enough, though not in the graces of social aptitude or dress sense. He took almost as much shit as Jack; a short little butter-ball, snug in his hand-knitted granny sweaters and pants that pulled too tight at his waist and swung too high at his ankles. Jack had to admit Toby could be a social dunce sometimes, because he had a tendency to choke up in groups bigger than two. But though anti-social by nature, Jack had seen a fellow outsider in the boy, through circumstance if not through choice. Toby was someone who shared his disdain for the others.

"So…did you bring it?" Toby greeted him.

"Bring what?"

"You know."

"Sure, I brought it."

"Yeah right."

"I did."

"Okay then," Toby said, leaning on the wall by the gates of the school, folding his arms. "Let me see it."

"What… here? Why don't I just whip it out, dribble it on over to the basketball court there, right in the middle of them jocks, and see if I can shoot some hoops with it?"

Toby laughed. "Yeah, okay, so where is it?"

"Down my pants."

"Never mind. I don't want to know."

"I'm serious."

"Oh yeah?" Toby looked at Jack, his eyes narrowing. "How do I know it's not a big act, like the makeup and the graveyard threads?"

"You're right," Jack said. "Years of practice. Guess I do make for a sight when I enter a room. It's Halloween fuck face, and you aren't wearing a costume."

Toby looked toward the football field, "Not that these people would ever notice."

Jack turned to look at Toby, but he was still watching everyone else.

"They notice," Jack assured him, surveying the hordes, his gaze lingering briefly on Anica Chapman. Not brief enough for Toby not to see, however.

"You wish she would notice," Toby said. He saw her cleavage all but popping out of a tight witch costume.

"Who? Her? I couldn't give a shit about her."

"Dude, who do you think you're kidding?"

"Whatever," Jack scowled.

Jack and Toby went silent after that, standing on the threshold of the parking lot and watching their peers loitering near the front doors of the school. All of them dressed for Halloween. A harmless sight to everyone but Jack. To Jack, they were no more than animals waiting to be slaughtered.

"So who you going to pop first?" Toby asked.

"Who? Doesn't matter. I want to be surprised."

"There must be someone who really gets you," Toby gazed at a large, brutish boy sitting on a short wall that divided the tarmac of the main parking lot from a token strip of grass that flanked the assembly hall. "There. How about Davies?"

"That guy?" Jack watched the boy who sat hunched like a pit bull, no doubt with the equivalent IQ. "Sure. I remember when I first moved here he was always on my ass."

"Mine too."

Toby watched a couple making out.

"How about Hurley?" he asked. "I wouldn't mind seeing his face blown off."

"Man, that fucking cock wart? I swear to God, dumb as a fucking donkey. And a coward I bet," Jack said.

"Too hung up on those pretty-boy looks of his. It seems to work, though."

Jack nodded.

"He likes to kid himself he charms them. His circle-jerk friends affectionately label him the funny one. All he does is rip it out off people who aren't gonna talk back to him and his pillow-biting jock buddies. He wouldn't know wit if it came along and kicked him in the nuts."

A skateboard from one of the nearby kids rolled over a few yards from the boys' feet and both of them looked down at it uneasily. Neither was athletic and both had a tendency, in such situations, to send the board back in quite the opposite direction they intended.

Anica Chapman ran over, flushed and breathing heavy.

"A little help?"

Jack froze.

"What?"

"I was hoping one of you gentleman might help me," she said, breathless, smiling, eyebrows raised.

They stood a moment more, and then Toby ran to the board and booted it toward her. He was off the mark by a couple yards, but the board found its way back to the roadway.

Anica winked at Toby, turned around, and was just about to return to the game, when she halted, turned back and looked at Jack. For a second her expression was unreadable. Then she widened her eyes and looked straight into his. "So tell me. Is it true what they say? No one likes a clown at midnight?"

Jack nearly averted his eyes, but caught himself and instead tried his best to maintain his composure. He smiled through his clown makeup, and it was gruesome.

"Want to find out?"

From across the parking lot one of her friends called out, asking if Anica planned on spending the rest of the day discussing D&D with the nerds. Anica blinked.

"Well, maybe I should wait till after dark." She smiled.

Toby leaned back against the school wall, relaxed and shrank back down. Jack let out the breath he had been holding and watched as she walked off with her friends.

"You know something?" Jack asked.

"What's that?"

"She's the one. I want to her to be the first to die."

"What? You've got to be kidding me."

"If I can't fuck her, then I'm going to kill her." Jack said, although he doubted he'd ever be able to.

Kill her...then fuck her...you can shoot her in the head, right below the chin, so when you're deep inside her, she'll be smiling as if she's still alive, and you'll even be able to see what she's thinking.

"Going soft now, Toby? I saw you about to blow a load in your pants just now. She's the worst of them all, and she's going to be the first."

"Why would you want to kill a girl like that?"

Jack knelt down beside Toby and straightened his loose dark adornments. They sat for a while watching Anica, blonde hair bouncing, slender legs in the tightest costume Jack figured he had ever seen.

"You want to know why? Look at her." Jack pointed.

Another moment of silence.

"Hear what happened between her and Sid Sorenson?" Toby asked.

"Who's Sid Sorenson?"

"He was a senior last year, some rich kid, a total dick. One night at a party, he pulls a knife on Anica, tells her to lie back and drop her panties. So anyway, Anica locks his wrist up, breaks it in three places, kicks him so hard in the balls he was limping for a month, and ever the perfectionist, pulls a can of pepper spray from her purse and gives him a quick shot in the face while he's lying there clutching his nuts with a broken hand."

"Seriously?" Jack thought this sounded like a challenge. "She really kicked his ass like that?"

"Seriously."

* * *

Jack tossed and turned in his sleep.

* * *

The morning bell rang out across the schoolyard and people began filtering into the buildings, their faces all sullen now.

Jack got up, his long black clothes rippling in the cool breeze. He looked like a teenaged specter that had returned from some time in the school's dark murky past.

"You're not going to chicken outta this one are you, Jack? You'll go through with it?" Toby stood up beside him.

Jack had already started walking toward the looming, totalitarian building, his long hair and drab clothes flowing around him, his face a dizzying mess of colorful greasepaint, Toby followed after him.

"So? You pussying out or you actually going through with it?"

"Just shut up and watch."

Room 203 looked more like a lecture hall than a high school classroom. The school was well equipped and they had another two rooms just like it. With the rows of padded chairs ascending steadily toward the back, it could have been a movie theatre. Mr. Foster had all the room in the world at the front, with a large mahogany desk next to a rotational blackboard and plenty of space in front of that for him to pace and pontificate.

Jack and Toby sat about midway up on the far left by the windows, relatively isolated, half the seats still yet to be filled. They were on the second floor at the far end of the school's newest wing, and with windows along three walls the room was large, well lit and coolly refreshing, as the industrial HVAC unit hummed out re-circulated air.

For the most part, the media studies class—a new trial subject—sat in glum silence, faces slack with boredom. The only sounds were those still filing into the class, pens tapping here and there, and self-pitying sighs.

Jack Sanders sat, unable to focus on Mr. Foster, because to him the sound seemed deafening. There were all kinds of characters in class, Frankenstein monsters, witches, vampires, and the rest of the high school kids.

Jack's hand fiddled ceaselessly with his biro. He dropped it, bent to pick it up from under his desk, but it spun from his grasp and landed a few rows down. He decided to leave it on the floor. His hands played instead with the gun that lay concealed in his lap.

Jack knew media studies was a pretty pointless subject that probably wouldn't exist in ten years time and certainly wouldn't get you anywhere in the real world, but it appealed to the theatrical side of him. He wanted to be an actor. Most of the other students chose it because they were too dumb to handle anything else or because their friends were doing the same thing. Right now, media studies was the "in" thing. If someone's general preference differed from that of the majority of his peers, they would change it accordingly.

A group of stoners strolled into the room, not portraying anything for Halloween but themselves, and headed toward the back. Jack wondered why they felt a need to dress, act, and be like each other, even if they strived to be different from the rest of the kids in the room. For them to assert their unique cultural identity it seemed necessary to have as much unification within their own crowd as possible. As Jack surveyed the seated student body—preppies sitting with preppies, cheerleaders with cheerleaders, stoners with stoners—they were all one in the same that day, all dressed for Halloween.

They will all die the same.

He, and perhaps Toby, were the only real people there that day. Yet they were hated or unnoticed for it.

Class was starting and the doors had been closed, though the seats near Jack and Toby remained vacant. Despite the absence of standing or moving bodies, the noises of the room seemed louder than ever to Jack.

Tap. Tap. Tap.

The creak of seats from people shifting weight.

Whispers.

The wall clock added its own beat to the music as it counted off the seconds.

Tick tock. Tick tock.

To Jack, it was a cacophony of sounds. He still couldn't hear a word from the teacher, who seemed oblivious to all but the sound of his own voice. Jack's hands shook and he clenched his fists. He stole glances around the classroom and saw groups of people, subdued, slack-jawed. He closed his eyes, cutting out the classroom. The sounds were as loud as ever.

He tried to calm himself, steady his breathing, but his body betrayed him and he couldn't keep track of his galloping heartbeat. His hand trembled on the gun. His palms were moist with sweat and the gun felt slick beneath his stroking fingers. No longer able to ignore the noise or calm the palpitations in his chest, he slid his hand around the gun, stood, raised the weapon, and yelled, "Freeze!"

He immediately felt stupid. Legs akimbo, pointing the gun around the room, with dry, cool, witty phrases like 'freeze' and dressed like Ronald McDonald on a bad day.

What a stupid thing to say.

Though most of his classmates had yet to realize what was happening, Jack could imagine them laughing at him, thinking of him as stupid, not in the least scared of a faceless loser, despite the weapon he wielded. All at once, white-hot fury boiled his blood and he shot the gun three times at the ceiling.

The room erupted. The same time the shots were fired and plaster fell from the ceiling, screams shattered the silence, people shot out of their seats in surprise, others were hit on the head by falling debris, and papers, pens, pencils, erasers, sharpeners, folders, books, and condoms scattered like exploding mortar off upturned desks.

"Sit the fuck down! I mean it. Sit the fuck down now."

The room was in an uproar. The frenzy grew worse and either no one heard him or they were all dumb as donkeys.

Mr. Foster bellowed Jack's name, and he turned to face his teacher, his sweat-riddled hair stinging his eyes and blurring his vision. All he saw was his mother in those eyes.

"Put the gun down, Jack," Mr. Foster said.

Jack didn't move.

"Give it to me."

Jack did as the teacher asked and put a bullet in his head. The old man's face twisted in surprise; his head snapped left as his arms flew up in the air. Foster's brains added brilliant touches of creativity to his name scrawled across the blackboard in heavy chalk. The blood trailed down around Foster's gore. Pieces of skull stuck to the day's teachings. The bullet went right through the corner post of the television set they were scheduled to watch a Birth of a Nation *on.*

When Jack told the class to shut up and sit down this time, they heard and they obeyed, but it wasn't silent. A number of girls shook and sobbed uncontrollably, a few heroic jocks half sat, half stood, in a poised crouch above their seats as if considering whether to rush Jack or maybe rush for the door, but they were smart and didn't make a move. Most were motionless, shocked, wide-eyed, and frightened.

Jack surveyed the chaotic scene—now so still, caught in time, as if by the flash of a camera, rather than the flash of a gun. Like forty deer all trapped in headlights. He had done the impossible. He had stripped every last one of them of the pretence, of their veneer, and with the façade gone, underneath, they were nothing more than scared, helpless animals. Jack pitied them in that moment. He looked to the wet blood that stained the blackboard, the mahogany desk, and the wall at the front of the classroom. He looked to the corpse, the head decimated, pouring forth red and brown gore. He closed his eyes and swallowed, turning back toward his classmates. In the past, when he dreamt about such a situation, he had thought of a thousand things to say, but now no words came. What was the point anyway? He just wanted to let his anger pour out of the barrel.

"Who wants to go first?"

No one said a word. He felt a shuddering against his leg, and when he looked down, he was surprised to see Toby looking up at him through his Coke bottle glasses, shaking and pale. The fear on his face was the same as everyone else's.

"My god, Jack," Toby said, barely audible, "You really brought it in. You really did it."

Jack hated Toby less then he hated anyone else there, but he had come here to relieve himself and this was as good a place to start as any.

"You want to die today, Tobes?"

"Oh god, no," Toby whispered, face white and lips trembling.

"Want to go first, buddy?"

Toby looked up at Jack's clown face, into his cold eyes, and had no idea what he was peering into. The fear of a bullet through his skull and his own wilting mortality squeezed the words in.

Jack lowered the gun, lining it up with the other boy's head.

"Goodbye, Toby. Time to finish. The final call. You've stepped up to the stage for your last bow, and I'm drawing the curtain."

The gunshot rang out like a thunderclap, heralding a rain of blood—and Jack fell to the ground.

* * *

"Jack!" Mikey yelled.

Jack sprang up on the couch, his breathing heavy. It was late, and it was no longer a dream. He had dreamt of that day over and over again as a teenager, and that day had been real, but he never got a chance to kill anyone. There had been a fire drill that day, but what really stopped him from going to prison was the fact he'd forgotten to bring bullets.

"What the hell happened?" Jack asked.

"You were dreaming," Mikey said.

"Jesus Christ…what a nightmare."

"What was it about?" Mikey asked.

"School…there was this kid…named Toby. Toby Halston. I saw him after graduation a few times; he went on to become a cop or something. But we were going to make a name for ourselves that day."

Jack sat up and lit a cigarette; he drank stale beer from a bottle beside the couch, careful not to swallow the cigarette butt floating at the bottom.

"There's still time." Mikey smiled.

"Yeah…" Jack stood, walked into the small kitchen and across the living room to the second family room, where doubled up Hefty bags filled with their latest star were spread across a bench. Jack walked by it, scratching his ass. He went to the kitchen and opened the fridge.

"Goddamn, I'm hungrier than Terry Schaivo."

Chapter Fourteen

"Have you ever been in love?" Mikey was leaning up against the barren wall, a poster of Sid Vicious wearing a swastika around his neck above him.

"Love?" Jack asked.

This kid had an abrupt way of asking questions.

"I think you know what I mean," Mikey said.

Jack came back in the room, laying a piece of stale hoagie aside. He pulled on a pair of jeans with blood still drying on the edge of the pockets. He lit a cigarette, parked it between two fingers and gobbled at the rock-hard hoagie roll.

"She was the woman of my dreams," Jack said. "She was so perfect."

"Really?"

"Yeah...I think we all have at least one girl like that in our lives, but what the fuck...life isn't worth living if you're already dead. I used to think it was the goth bitch I met in rehab, but it goes further back than that.

"It was the summer after senior year, the year I moved out here. It was a Tuesday. I had an office job while I was looking for acting work. Some new temps were brought in for the holidays to help with filing. And on that Tuesday, on the way back from a coffee break, I saw *her*. She was the most beautiful woman I'd ever seen; short brown hair, Lisa Loeb glasses and this fucking radiance that just oozed from her. I walked by and caught her out of the corner of my eye. I stopped short and spilled coffee all over myself. I was just staring at her as she sat there, filing away. I couldn't move, and finally, she looked up at me, flashed this smile, and looked back down. The smile snapped me out of it. I fumbled for words but came up blank.

"When I got back to my desk, I just sat there. My cubicle was only two or three down and across the aisle from her. If I leaned back just far enough, I could see her. Her back was to me, but I knew she was still there. A couple of times, I could have sworn she was looking over her shoulder at me, but I figured it was my mind playing tricks. I didn't get much work done that day, for obvious reasons, but I watched her. Closely. I had wonderful fantasies about me and her and a bottle of blue cheese dressing. I wanted the taste of her pussy on my lips. I wanted her to bleed into my mouth for days. I wanted to smell her panties and then shove them in her mouth while I paved the roads of her thighs. I wanted to fuck her so hard her father would feel it in his balls."

"So what happened?" Mikey asked.

"She got up at one point and came back about fifteen minutes later. I didn't think much of it. When quitting time rolled around, and I saw people packing up and leaving, I glanced at my clock in disbelief. Had it really been five hours since lunch? Had I really missed a break? It certainly didn't seem that way, but it explained the fifteen minutes she disappeared. When I saw her put on her coat— a long, black woolen number that made her seem even more beautiful—I sprang into action. I dumped all my papers into the top drawer of my desk and threw my coat on. She was halfway down the hall when I got out of my cubicle and I caught up with her by the elevators. As I pulled up next to her I had her attention. I knew I had to say something…

"Hey."

"I, uh, I saw you working today."

"I saw you seeing me."

"Yeah, uh, I was wondering…could I, and if this is forward just let me know, could I get your number?"

Jack chewed on the last of the hoagie.

"She stopped dead in her tracks, but then she grabbed me by the wrist, pulled my hand toward her, and scribbled down seven digits."

"What was her name?" Mikey asked.

"Amanda."

"Did you call her?"

"Yeah, I called her. The perfect girl had just given me her phone number.

"I got into my car and sped home, through the rainy night. I wanted to call her right when I got home, but didn't want to seem desperate, so I waited. And waited. And waited. It was eight thirty. I stared at the phone. It was nine. I'd been staring at the phone for a half hour. Maybe I was weird. Eventually, I decided TV might take my mind off this woman I knew nothing about.

"Anyway, I settled in to watch it, and must have fallen asleep, because I woke up the next afternoon on the couch. It was twelve thirty, and I was three and a half hours late for work. I raced to the bathroom and got a good look at myself in the mirror. I looked like dog shit after it's dried in a bitter winter with no precipitation. You ever see that Mikey?"

"No."

"It's white…. black shit turns white in the winter, but I digress…Anyway, my hair was all buzzed off back then, I was half-shaven and my mouth tasted like a stripper's asshole. I brushed my teeth, grabbed a comb and razor, straightened my tie, and busted out the door. I had an old station wagon with more rust on it then a dead cripple's leg braces. I was going at a decent clip, stopping only for red lights, when I'd comb my hair and shave. Then I saw blue and red lights in my rearview.

'Fuck!'

"I pulled over."

'License and registration, please.'

"I obliged, but I did imagine stabbing him with the pen sitting in the ashtray under the tape deck. He was crotch-level with the window. I'd stab him in the balls with it and play hell with his vas deferens for a while. Then wear his badge to work."

'Do you know why I pulled you over?'

'Yes, officer,' I did my best 'elementary school student being forced to say good morning teacher' voice.

'Well then, maybe you could explain the rush you were in.'

'I'm late to work.'

'How late?'

'Three and a half hours.'

'Well, shit, son. I'll write you out a warning this time, but next time, set a damn alarm.'

"I drove away and breathed a sigh of relief. I couldn't believe that worked, but it was one by now. I said fuck it. I'd rather call in sick and take the day off then get to work and just get bitched at the rest of the day. My only real reason for going was to see Amanda, anyway. I thought back to the smile she gave me as she wrote down her number on my hand. At six, I picked up the phone and dialed. I suddenly tensed up. What the fuck was I going say? She picked up.

'Hello?'

'Hi, Amanda?'

'That's me. Who's this?'

'This is Jack…Jack Sanders.'

'Oh, hi! I didn't see you at work today.'

I didn't go.'

'Oh.'

'So, uh, do you want to go out some time?'

'Sure.'

'How about Friday?'

'Sounds good.'

'Excellent.'

"I heard the click and thought how surprisingly well it had all gone. I was excited. So excited, in fact, that I ran around my house singing some old Beatles' song my foster mom used to play all the time. Thinking back to that now, Mikey…I probably should've done the world a favor and hung myself right along side of my foster mother."

"So then what?" Mikey watched Jack spray his Jeans with Oxiclean. Jack wondered if that fat, bearded fuck that does all the commercials ever used the shit on brain stains and arterial blood before. There is a difference. Arterial blood is thick and clotty, much harder to get out of two-hundred dollar designer jeans.

"The next two days were a whirlwind. On Thursday, we'd gone on breaks together and talked and laughed. We hammered out the details of our first date as well. It was going to be the picture of perfection, a fucking X-rated Norman Rockwell painting. She would come to my place and then there'd be dinner and a movie. On Friday, work was another blur. More breaks, more talking, more laughing. I ducked out early, though. I wanted to make sure everything would be ready for that night. I was giddy by the time the doorbell rang. She was early and I wasn't ready yet, but it didn't matter, because when I opened the door, and saw her standing there, illuminated by my dim porch light, I thought I had never seen anyone so beautiful. So perfect. That's when I buried the axe in her skull."

Mikey coughed up cigarette smoke. He saw Jack's gaze against the window where thick stains of tobacco tar had collected.

"She was so perfect. Better to keep it that way," Jack said. His eyes were listless. "We better get moving Mikey. We've got to dump the body."

* * *

Let's be frank here, Jack thought, *when does the dissertation to hope end? Is it as long as a rope? Could I still feel my foster mother choking to death?*

Jack no longer cared about Melanie Sanders. With every girl, especially the bitch he had tortured and pretended to play dentist on, he cared even less. Adoption is like pity, a word without judgment. He pitied no one and judged all.

Just like mom…
Just like Amanda…

The GTO had a busted radiator the night Jack took Mikey to East L.A. Their latest customer would be hovered over the side of the porcelain and foaming bubbles in a blood bath by now, screaming and crying over his wife's slashed open arm. She cut right through the bracelets of fortune, down to where things made the most sense, in the purple, in the lost.

In the snuff…

"I'm done with all this soon." Mikey looked at Jack, who seemed overdressed tonight. His shirt was black and the tie a deep maroon, the color of blood clots. He smiled over at Mikey as if his mouth was filled with razor blades.

On the radio, Zeppelin sang about going to California. When the song ended, a voice came on briefly with a news report. The body of a young actress was found floating face down near the Rockport Tunnel, about twenty miles from where Jack's car now rolled down an alley.

"What the fuck are you talking about, Mike?" Jack asked. "Why quit now?"

"It's gone too far. I'm done"

"How far is that?" Jack's eyes darted to the passenger's seat.

"How far are you willing to go with this? Eventually we're going to get caught."

"The good ones never get caught," Jack said. "They just give up."

"Enough. You knew it had to end eventually."

"I'm not the one trying to probe the mind through the asshole," Jack said. "I know what I want when I go down in it, and I see everything the way it was meant to be."

Mikey lit a cigarette while Jack shifted gears. The rain outside was merciless as they slowed to a halt beside the alley apartment.

"It's over for me," Mikey said.

"Shut the fuck up and get out of my car. When have you ever had a sense of clemency? When the fuck has your moral compass been anything but skewed?"

"I'm just tired of it all," Mikey said, and Jack saw the truth in his friend's eyes. It wasn't like all those girls. It was different. It was genuine, real, and it scared Jack. It was like looking at himself before all this began; before he had left home, before his foster mother, before all of it.

Mikey's eyes looked like his own when his career was winding down, long since stagnant. They say dentists have the highest suicide rates, but Jack would be damned to believe in that long moment he saw Mikey's raw honesty, if it wasn't actors.

"Goodnight." Mikey stepped out of the car.

Jack didn't have time for regrets.

* * *

The nightclub was called *The Cobra Spine* and already had a line as long as Amanda's unraveled intestines. He saw what the entire world had to offer strung together like ropes of bleeding flesh. They stood like soldiers, fake tits and collagen, with gums still bleeding from the latest outpatient procedure. The doctors out here were all the same, all from the same circus. The result was the same too—bleached-blond ex-trailer trash in Dolce and Gabbana. Armani clad whores. The men, the women, the whole mess was one clusterfuck that continually devolved. No matter what the label says, the come stains are still hard to get out and the blood never washes away.

Pulling up to the club, Jack killed the engine and took in the silence. He sat in awe of the outside world, hearing the rain pelt against the roof and seeing the shaky, violent scene through streams of wavy water. The palm trees in Los Angeles, the humidity, the city lights, none of it mattered. He was a root among dead weeds, avoiding the chemicals called life, and his dick got hard at the thought of taking that whole line right out of the picture.

Jack exited the car, walking through the rain, as his dark hair hung in his face, dripping with polluted water and mixing with shampoo he had used to wash last night's work off of his scalp. Things had gone so well; he had had pieces of her birth canal stuck to his forehead. The bouncer waved Jack on, and he butted to the dead of the velvet rope.

"Been a long time."

"So it has," Jack said.

"Someone wants to talk to you."

"I know big man…Miller called me."

"How do you know Miller?" the bodyguard asked.

"Old friends."

Yeah, friends… the motherfucker sold himself out to the big leagues, leaving me behind doing movies for the fucking Sci-Fi Channel.

"You can go in," the bouncer said, "but it isn't Miller…"

"What do you mean?"

"This guy wants to talk business. He went through Miller to get you, but you didn't hear it from me."

"Thanks," Jack said.

Walking into the front lounge was always doomed for Jack. So many memories of coke whores and midnight parties, drinking anisette out on the deck of another run down motel. Being invited to A-list functions out of pity, where actresses and actors alike blow their way to the top and spread their legs just the same. Who were they kidding? A porn star and a movie star are one in the same. The industry needed fresh faces and real fear. The essence of drama is in the struggle.

Jack pushed his way through the layers of smoke and perfume and sweat. Flesh smoothing out and folding. Sparkles and shine, drinks and wine, and nothing but failure was here tonight. One big giant fucking cesspool of havebeens and have-nots. The girls were faux beautiful and the men were anxious.

Walking slowly, the music was loud and pulsed in the back of his neck as he walked along the snakeskin railing that Miller Vance, asshole extraordinaire, had installed a few years ago. He played his games in Hollywood and used this place to pay the bills, just like Jack was doing. Paying the bills was a good way of looking at it. Keeping the economy moving. Letting the cash trickle down with the blood.

Reagan would have been proud.

A girl in a tube top and leather miniskirt, snakeskin of course, strolled up to him, a tray of assorted drinks in one hand. Miller had called him earlier, while Mikey was digging, but now there was a hint of mystery to the call. He was told to wear a suit. No one in the Cobra Spine wore suits accept the bouncers.

"You Jack?" the waitress asked.

"Depends on who I'm fucking."

"Well…" The waitress's eyes widened. "Mr. Vance, left this for you."

Jack was staring at the envelope in the woman's hand. His eyes drifted down to it, then back at the waitress's young face.

"Where is Miller, by the way?"

"You better just read the letter," she said. "Want a beer?"

"Heineken," Jack said. "And a shooter."

"Whiskey?"

"Whatever you feel like baby."

Jack watched her walk away; her ass in that skirt was like watching two kittens fighting underneath silk sheets. He tore the envelope open with the same folding buck knife that had become a staple in his most recent films and opened the note inside.

Jackie boy…

It's been, what, two years since we've seen each other? I got a little problem, Jack, and I need your help. I know you probably want to kill me for leaving you high and dry, but do me a favor and be there for me one more time.

There's a duffle bag in my office upstairs. It has $50,000 in it. It's yours if you do what the man downstairs says. You'll know him when you see him. He's wearing a suit. You and him are probably the only motherfuckers in here wearing a suit, and I made that happen on purpose. His name is Raymond Garretti. He's Italian and connected. He knows what you're all about. So do I, and so do a few other key players. Don't worry, no one will say a thing; we got your back. You don't think we'd give up a profit like that do you? No, Jack, we protect our interests, and our interests are you and the freak that's been helping you.

You see, you made a film for a member of the Brotello gang a few weeks ago. He's a member of a ring in New York. Garretti has been warring with him for years now. He wants you to make a film for him starring a few of Brotello's girls.

Trust me, you want to do this. This film is worth two things you've been looking for.

Garretti's boys are willing to pay you half a million for the movie.

And if you do this for me, my bar stays open and I'll get you back into starring in real films, better than the bit parts and straight to DVD shit you were doing before.

I hope we can be friends again.

Miller-

Jack lowered the note, and then crumbled it into a ball with his left hand, making a fist. This was one thing he didn't want to happen, and it went right back to robbing the Mexican restaurant and the first film. When it started getting big, everyone wanted a piece. Jack walked through the crowd while Trent Reznor sang about his crown of shit over the house system. He saw the only man that could be Raymond Garretti.

The man sitting in a shadowy back booth with brandy flavored ice melting in front of him saw Jack and raised his glass. His smile was all buisness.

The mobster stood, hand out, still smiling at Jack. "Jack Sanders?"

"That would be me," Jack said cautiously.

"Please sit; we have some business to discuss."

Turn back now Jack, Jack thought. *Take off, fuck this…you can hide out for a while. You and Mikey have made enough money in the last four months to just hang out in the Bahamas for a while.*

Jack knew that wouldn't work. He could hide from the cops, but no one hides from the mob. They're the best moles in the world, and the places they dig always lead to rivers of blood.

"So what's this all about?" Jack asked.

"No rush my friend," Garretti said. "Enjoy yourself, drinks are on the house. Where's your co-star? Your friend?"

"That's funny," Jack laughed. "I don't have any friends."

"Everybody has friends," Garetti smiled. "It's hard to get by without them."

Raymond Garretti was a good man. Sure, he got caught up in some bad situations, but a good man nonetheless. A gambling problem followed him everywhere, however. He was a 44-year old hitter, twice divorced.

Garretti had done a lot of good for California, donating to charities.

Killing preachers who didn't pay up…

Starting a local Little League for kids…

Collecting money to fund it, with fake t-bill funds, then killing anyone who started asking questions…

He even helped set up a free drug clinic…

And the counselors just so happened to run the same drugs for Garretti and his dogs that they tried to wean the patients off of…

Garretti had buried a lot of people's troubles...

And he'd buried a lot of people with them...

"Hungry?"

"No thanks," Jack said.

"Okay...so I guess we should get down to it then." Garretti reached in his jacket pocket and pulled out a cigar. He bit one end and lit the other.

"Back when I was seven or eight, I had my first taste of gambling, Jack. My friend Oscar Chi, he's dead now—wife killed him with a pair of scissors—was a big baseball fan and he just knew the Red Sox would win the '86 World Series. I didn't know much about baseball, but I accepted Oscar's proposition to bet ten dollars that the Red Sox would lose. They did. The New York Mets won, and I was $10 richer. Ever since then, gambling was my new hobby. But I don't bet on anything I can lose, and that's why I'm betting on you."

"What do you mean?" Jack asked.

"I mean, I want you to make a film for me, for *us*, and I'll pay you five-hundred grand to do it. Whatever you need, you've got. I've heard about your work but didn't think about it much until I saw one of your DVDs. You're a sick fuck. If I didn't know any better, I'd hire you to take down some of my ...well, problems, but I digress.

"The specifics have been worked out already. I have four girls waiting. I want you to make your masterpiece, Jack, one that will never be forgotten. I want carnival and carnage, you know, like a fucking funhouse?"

"You're kidding."

"I don't joke about business," Garretti said. "It's a thing that hell has no place for."

"Hell has a place for us all," Jack said.

"I sense you don't trust me, so let me tell you something."

"What's that?"

"I'm the only person you *can* trust."

"Is that so?"

"You don't know me," Garretti said. "So let's not pretend. Money will keep us friends."

"Money is a good friend." Jack watched Garretti lean forward, his big nose shining under the dancing strobes. He had a cautious disposition, almost as if he wanted to say something precarious but changed his mind.

"I knew this guy named Ritchie Ryan, a real piece of shit, but he was the ideal bookie, an old Mick with slicked back gray hair and enough money to own half of Los Angeles. I felt confident about this guy, and he could get an easy forty grand off anyone in the business. One year during a big scam, I placed a bet with Ritchie that the Celtics would cover a four-point spread against Chicago. I thought it was an easy forty grand, but the Bulls won by ten, and I didn't have the forty grand. Truth be told, I only had about $100 to my name.

"He told me I had two weeks to get him the money, and since Ritchie wasn't the kind of guy to joke about anything, especially when it came to money, I didn't have much of a choice but to find some way to come up with $40,000."

"Why are you telling me this?" Jack asked.

"You're friend...Mikey..."

"What about him?" Jack asked.

"First, I robbed a convenience store." Garretti ignored the question. "It was sheer luck I got away with it; I'd never tried something so obvious before and hoped I'd never have to again. I walked out of that 7-11 with twelve-hundred dollars that I didn't have walking in, but I was still nowhere near what I needed. I needed something bigger but had no idea what. I decided to take up pick pocketing. I knew it wouldn't get me everything I needed, but it might help me along while I thought of something else.

"Anyway, I had a week and a half left to get the money, and I was in a little diner in Newton eyeing a young guy who had a fat stack of bills in his wallet when he got up to pay. The guy had mayonnaise from a B.L.T all over his greasy mouth, and I didn't really want to get near him. But hey, you got to do what you got to do, right?"

"Yeah." Jack swallowed what was left of his beer.

"So, when the guy got up and walked toward the cash register at the end of the counter, I got up too. I mumbled an 'excuse me' as I bumped into him, and the guy never noticed his wallet was gone. I waited until he left and sat back down in one of the booths. The fat stack turned out to be all ones. The fucking idiot didn't even have a credit card. Just a goddamn driver's license that had the picture of some college fag with a dope fuck hat. I still remember his name, Mike Freeman."

"Mike Freeman?" Jack suddenly perked up.

"Yes," Garretti said. "Know him don't you?"

"Usually only as Mikey."

"Small world isn't it?" Garretti asked.

"Sure is."

"Anyway, I was sitting there counting money, and some greasy fuck came up behind me rolling a toothpick between his lips."

"*Nice move there, kid.* I knew right away he was a cop …a perfect end to a fucked up day. I handed the wallet over, and told him I'd give it back to the guy. He was still outside, and I begged him to let me go. He just told me to shut up and follow him."

"What does this have to do with Mikey?" Jack asked.

Garretti waved for the closest girl with a tray of drinks and looked at Jack.

"Please don't interrupt me…I'm telling a story here…you got someplace you gotta be?"

"Guess not."

"Good." Garretti smiled. "So anyway, I followed the guy out to his car. He was a good-looking guy, with a leather jacket and jet black hair, probably around 40 or so. I was a lot younger and stupider then, and he made me nervous. When we got to the guy's car, he got in the driver's side and I sat down in the passenger's seat. He introduced himself as John Memphis and asked me what I was doing. I told him about my gambling problem, and about Ritchie Ryan, and the convenience store, and everything. When I finished, he didn't say anything a long time.

"When he finally spoke, he told me about this family in New York. Nice family—ma, pa, kid—but the father just happened to be the one and only Mr. Brotello and had a few extra grand sitting around the house. He told me we'd split the money right down the middle. I realized I didn't really have a choice. Later on, he tells me that to get the money, we'll need to break into his house and get the combination to the safe. So I ask him what the safe looks like, and he tells me it looks like a clown's head."

"That's fucked up," Jack said, "but what about Mikey? I don't understand."

Garretti leaned forward. "Understand this, you twisted bastard. I'm going to finish this story if it takes me all night. You see those two guys over there by the girls dancing in the corner?"

Jack looked and saw two tall men in Hawaiian shirts.

"Yeah."

"Good. If you fuck with me, I'll have them take care of your friend Mikey. We know where he lives, so don't fuck with us. I got four girls for you to use, and you're going to make this movie."

"If they're going willingly, I'm assuming these aren't your girls?"

Garretti smiled. "Never mind that for now."

The waitress saddled up to the table, and Garretti looked up and smiled. "Bring my friend here whatever he wants, and another brandy for me darling."

The waitress returned the smile.

"Another Heineken," Jack said.

"So back to my story…where was I? Oh yeah, so I'm sitting in this car and this scary fucker tells me to meet him at this same diner tomorrow at noon. From there, we'd take a train into Greenwich and go our separate ways for the day.

"Sitting in my apartment that night, watching the late night movie, I tried to take my mind off what I'd agreed to, but it did no good. The doorbell rang, and I trudged to the door and unlatched it. A blond man stumbled in, wearing dirty clothes and a cowboy hat. His hair was a mess and reeked of alcohol. He had blood on one corner of his mouth and tears in his eyes. He was ready to pass out, and I helped him to the sofa. I wiped the hair out of his face, and I recognized him. It was the cocksucker on the ID from the wallet I lifted earlier."

"Mikey?" Jack asked.

"Yeah…" Garretti said. "Fucking Mikey."

"So, Mikey was somehow connected to you guys?"

"Yeah," Garretti said. "Your buddy owes Brotello a lot of money. Brotello has no idea who ripped him off, but the three of us broke into his house and stole all the cash out of that ugly clown head. Brotello killed a lot of my friends trying to figure it out, so I want this to be personal, Jack. I want these four girls to wear clown makeup, a fucking fun house scene, got it?"

"Yeah." Jack said.

"Good…I've already got a place ready for you"

"I don't do things that way," Jack said. "I'll come get the girls, wherever you want, and I'll bring them back to the movie set. If I'm followed, the deal is off, and if anything happens to Mikey, I'll make sure the next movie I make has *you* in it."

Garretti looked at Jack and smiled again.

Chapter Fifteen

Outside, the rain ended but Jack was just getting started. He had a slip of paper in his pocket with an address on it—462 Brunswick Avenue. That's where the girls were waiting.

He'd go back to tell Mikey and get the set ready. A circus scene would take some preparation, but with Mikey along, it could be fun.

I'm done...

Mikey wasn't done, but he did have a lot on his mind.

As Jack headed east—*The Cobra Spine* shrinking in his rearview mirror—he tried to reach Mikey on his cell. Nothing. He thought about heading back to the house but decided the bar was probably a better call. He was wrong.

Mikey was at home, slumped on the couch with a bottle of Jack Daniels. He hated the name Jack, even as he stared at the famous black and white label. Some infomercial was on the television and tears were waiting to dry on Mikey's face. What had happened last night reminded him of something he would never tell Jack.

Too busy staring into the amber blur of the whiskey, he never heard the front door softly open. As prices on the screen were slashed again and again and a cigarette butt smoldered in the overflowing ashtray at Mikey's feet, someone approached. His thoughts once hollow with memory, now thick with surprise, as something cold pressed up against the side of his head, where that bitch had slapped him last night. That bitch that would never slap anyone again. He knew it was a gun barrel. He heard the click of the hammer.

"Hello, Mikey," a voice spoke. The rain outside pelted the windows.

"My wallet is on the desk. Everything I've got is in there."

"I don't want your money, Mikey," the voice said. "I want to make a *movie.*"

Chapter Sixteen

Jack threw the cell phone across the deserted factory floor. Mikey still wasn't answering, and he needed him now more than ever. It was hard convincing the four beauties waiting outside that this audition for a porn film would get them hired, but he made up a bullshit excuse, and as always, it worked. That was part of being an actor. Another part was knowing when to shut the fuck up.

He took his time, first with the blonde, painting her face up like a clown and giving her a red ball nose. She wore baggy electric-blue silk clown pants and nothing at all up top. The rainbow suspenders cut dead center along her nipples and went over her shoulders.

The redhead's pale face was painted half black, half white—a harlequin. She wore a silky blouse and nothing else.

The third "actress" was a twenty-something black girl from Seattle. She told Jack her acting career had come to a halt when she got pregnant. Jack painted her face like a skull and gave her a blue clown nose. She was excited but worried about the C-section scar on her abdomen. Jack assured her that they'd take care of it during final cut.

The fourth girl, a raven-haired Italian, was painted white, her clown nose as red as Jack's own. Jack giggled right along with her when he painted her areolas. The paintbrush tickled her, and he wondered how tickled she'd be when he dug deep into her tits with a box cutter.

Where the fuck is Mikey?

What was once a warehouse was now an empty party room.

The beginning and end of something great.

Jack had replaced the wallpaper with the bare necessities. He'd spent the past few hours playing Martha Stewart, cleaning and sponging the floors, clearing the cobwebs. He bought bright red, white, and blue Mylar balloons, colors that matched his makeup. A pile in the corner contained what seemed like every bag of cotton candy in the metropolitan area. That day sophomore year had been the last time he had worn makeup, but tonight would be something of a private reunion.

The starlets were seated on the bed, two stained mattresses covered in colorful children's bedding. Balloons were everywhere. Beside the bed was a popcorn machine, along the far wall, the stacks of pink and baby blue cotton candy. Sharp, spun sugar ecstasy.

Around the bed on a circular track ran a model train. The cameras, the lighting, everything was set. Jack opened the tray of CD player and popped in Tom Waits' *Black Rider*.

"What the fuck is that?" Vanessa's black skin shone like chocolate under the hot halogen lights.

"With everything going on right now, the music is what bothers you?" Jack asked, genuinely curious. Even through his wild face paint, his expression was both innocent and fresh, dark and brooding. It made his eyes look like bleeding lines of silver mercury.

"Never mind," she said.

"I think it sounds cool." The dark haired girl with painted tits smiled. Jack had given her bleeding mascara. It looked like she'd been crying all day, her eyes some strange kind of misplaced stigmata.

"Time to start."

"Why do I feel ...woozy?" the blonde asked.

"Me too. What the fuck did you...slip us?"

"Now why would God do that to his angels?" Jack smiled. His grin stretched ear-to-ear, but in truth, things were getting blurry sooner than he had planned. He'd given them all a beer, laced with Rohypnol.

The circus has come to town.

Lucky Day Overture finished. *The Black Rider* began.

"All right ladies, if we can start," Jack looked through the viewfinder of the camera on the tri-pod. "Just as we discussed. Are we ready?"

"Ready when you are, baby," the blonde cooed. Her tits were perky, ready to cut glass.

The girls began, kissing one another and pressing their now sweaty flesh together. It did nothing for Jack, but when the blonde bent over and faceplanted herself in a snatch, he saw the curvature of her spine and lost what was left of his mind.

As Vanessa gobbled the swollen clitoris of the redhead, Jack entered the circus. He got behind Vanessa; her black skull makeup already melting. From behind, Jack-O the Clown strapped a ball gag on her face. She gladly accepted it. The ball gag was filled with holes so it could drain. Jack began by spitting on her from behind, then pushing in her, his cock peeking through the curtain of his clown pants.

Jack saw the scar from her episiotomy, from where the doctor didn't have a wide enough pussy to pull little Timmy through, where a man is given his stretch of skin to prevent him from shitting on his own nuts. He realized she just wasn't wet enough and slit open her taint to the pink beneath. Blood gushed; it ran down the crack of her pussy and dribbled on the floor.

"How about a candy apple?" Jack whispered. He continued to fuck Vanessa while she screamed. He pulled her backward, but the redhead didn't notice. She was working on her own clit while her arm rested beneath those massive tits of hers. Her nipples were olive colored. Her lips were full and wet. Both sets.

Vanessa tried to scream through her ball gag. Spit flew in strings from her mouth. From behind, Jack was balls deep inside her, and before he came for the first time, he held a box cutter in front of her face and slid the button up, releasing the stubby razor blade. Vanessa's eyes lit up at the sight of it. Her skull makeup was a mess and about to get messier.

"I should've killed you all the day I had the chance," Jack laughed, the sound of coyotes and maniacs sharing the same moon.

Jack slit Vanessa's left cheek with the blade, as she shook and screamed. Blood pattered on the bed beneath her. Some of it peppering the redhead's bare feet. Jack brought the blade down again, this time on Vanessa's right cheek. The greasepaint running into the deep lacerations made her crazy with pain. Her pussy tightened, and Jack was lost in the moment. He came again when he slashed her throat from ear to ear.

She died knowing he was right. Final cut didn't matter.

Vanessa was tossed to the side; her corpse finished bleeding while Jack fell on the redhead. Still oblivious, she tried to kiss him.

He pushed her away; she tasted of poison and reminded him of his mother. Instead, he grabbed a bag of cotton candy, tore it open with his teeth and shoved wads of it into her mouth. She giggled while it dissolved. The other two girls were busy with each other, and Jack slammed the redhead against the wall at the head of the bed. Her harlequin face was smearing, but the camera auto focused. He pinned her hands back with his knees and shoved his bloody cock into her cotton candy stuffed mouth. She sucked gallantly and swallowed him all the way. As she did, her mouth erupted with blue candy juice, and it ran down the length of Jack's thigh. He looked up at the ceiling while throat fucking her and suddenly understood that if there was a heaven it was this very moment.

Jack grabbed her by the hair and pulled her over to a hanging leather swing, riddled with straps and chains. With a little effort, Jack strapped her in it. Her feet were stretched far apart, her tits bounced and her clown face—now a wreck—shone under the hot lamps.

"I made this just for you," Jack said. He looked over at the camera. "Ready to get freaky, kids?"

He turned back toward the redhead and saw the hundreds of freckles along the inside of her thighs. Her clean-shaven pussy hung there like balaclava, and Jack began stuffing it with cotton candy. It melted immediately, and Jack pulled the swing close, tasting her twat for all it was worth.

Considering the situation, the redhead seemed to be enjoying herself, at least until Jack grabbed a Styrofoam box filled with bags of cubed dry ice. Pulling on a protective glove, he reached inside and grabbed two cubes. He stopped the swing.

"Shut your eyes angel," Jack said.

The girl did as she was told, and Jack placed a cube of dry ice on each eyelid. Before the pain started, he grabbed a few more cubes and shoved them inside her. Her uterus began to seize and burn. She tried opening her eyes to the pain but couldn't. Suddenly, she felt her candy-violated mouth pull open, and more cubes fell in against her throat and tongue.

Jack left her there, swinging in mid air, and made his way over to the two girls having fun on their own. He grabbed the girl on top, the blonde, and began shoving his cock down her throat. To her unpleasant surprise, it tasted of pre-cum, blood, and sweet sickness. His pubic hair was knotted with dried sugar spun into flavors unimaginable. She knew instantly that nothing in this room was forbidden. He pinched the blonde's nose.

"I'm going to kill you," Jack said. "How does that sound on a night like this? I think Anica was right, no one likes a clown at midnight."

The blonde's clown nose tumbled off her face, as Jack pushed the inside of her cheek in and out with the head of his dick. In seconds, he left her makeup dripping with come. She reared back and licked her fingers. Jack liked that. From the corner, he brought a portable helium tank and meat cleaver. He pulled the hose to the bedside as the Italian girl barely watched, the Rohypnol heavy in her bloodstream.

"What are you going to do?"

"You darling," Jack said. "Again and again."

Jack got on his knees, and while the blonde rested on hers, Jack took the meat cleaver and slammed it as hard as he could into her back. Her eyes lit up with shock, and she opened her mouth to scream. When she did, Jack forced her down onto her back, and began to stretch a balloon over her head. The girl went crazy, jerking out of control. As she jerked and spazzed, the cleaver buried itself deeper into her spinal column. Jack leaned over her.

"Can't breathe baby?"

He grabbed the air hose.

"Here…let me help you."

While holding her down by the throat, Jack popped the nozzle of the air hose through the blue latex. The metal of the hose broke her top front teeth. He fed it down her throat as she gagged and the gas filled her from the inside.

The girl in the swing screamed unmercifully.

Jack returned to her, her frantic movements moving the swing back and forth. Jack pushed his gloved fingers inside her cunt, grabbed the wad of dry ice and pulled. The woman screamed with her mouth closed and bleeding. Part of her uterus was stuck together in a wad as he pulled it free, tearing most of her labia away with it. Blood dripped on the floor as Jack began to mutilate her, thrusting in her with his fist. He put his bloody hand in her mouth, prying it open, and pulled the dry ice free from her throat and cheeks. Her tongue came with it. Jack began humming along with *Gospel Train*. When he pulled the ice off each closed eyelid, the flesh came along, eyelashes and all. Without any eyelids she didn't blink, not even when Jack pulled her head back and beat her to death with the remaining box of ice. Her head hung loosely off the swing, and Jack walked around it, catching his breath.

By now, the effects of the sedative had worn off a little on the dark-haired Italian, the one with the painted tits. Jack moved quickly. She was beginning to get up, stumbling for the door, but he grabbed a taser from beside the bed and hit her with it. She jiggled, went down, and when she came back to the harsh reality, she noticed her legs behind her head. Jack was fucking her hard. Her mouth was wedged open with a chrome clamp device. Jack went all over her body, from ass to mouth and back again. Her terrified eyes saw the dead women in the room. Jack came on her face, then grabbed a power drill with a saw bit used to make holes in doors for a knob to fit. Jack used it to put a hole in the Italian's forehead. As he began to trepan her, she screamed. Bits of bone dust and blood mist filled the air. It rained all over Jack's painted face, but he was careful not to go too deep, not to disrupt the brain. He used his fingernail to carefully pry off the perfect piece of scalp he had made, and saw the brilliant gray matter underneath, wet and shiny in the florescent light.

"Please...no..."

Jack only smiled and reached behind him, dropping the drill and grabbing a can of Comet bathroom cleaner. The cleanser was bluish and powdery.

"It's time to rid your mind of all this filth," Jack said.

She screamed, her eyes rolled up toward her forehead, desperately wanting to know what was being done to her. The pain had all but disappeared until Jack began dumping the cleaner into the perfect hole. It bubbled, sizzled, and expanded.

The Italian girl, Desmond would be her name in the obituaries, had a trip she wouldn't forget. A massive headache worse than any migraine engulfed her. She felt as though her brain had caught fire, yet, an odd, colorfuly-magnified sensation overwhelmed her. Her vision became that of colorblindness, then all red and blue. Jack dumped more Comet in and let her die as her head hung off the side of the bed. Trails of Comet dust falling to the floor like ashes, he finished fucking her. Even with no pulse, he didn't stop until he was done. She bit her tongue in half and swallowed it, because that was what a brain riddled with Comet would tell you to do.

When he was finished, and dropped her legs back on the bed, Jack stood in the room, his clown makeup now smeared and distressed. He looked around the room at the mayhem and never felt more proud. The last sounds of *Carnival* echoed from the walls of the warehouse.

It was true; no one liked a clown at midnight.

Chapter Seventeen

Back in town, Jack stopped by the house to look for Mikey.

It wasn't like him not to show up.

Jack left in the early evening, still no sign of Mikey. He figured they'd meet up later. It wouldn't be a problem; they would reconcile their differences. Sometimes it was just that easy.

Jack drove the twenty miles out to the beach, while the horizon bled with colors. Last night had been his magnum opus for sure. The sun was a blood orange needing peeled of its light. He saw the town car parked alone by the t-shirt shop. Jack rolled to a stop and sat among the stillness, gradually taking in the tranquility of the sun against his still oily skin. Jack had to admit, it felt good wearing it, even after he'd gone back to the girl in the swing, the one that reminded him of mom so much, and began to bite her. He bit off her nipples and swallowed them. Only, when his mouth couldn't take it anymore, when his jaw ached from his forceful bites, did he stop.

He had gnawed on her fingers while she was still alive, barely breathing with a broken neck. He had thought she was dead. A simple oversight. Just like not expecting to rob a restaurant and kill a pregnant woman. Just like not expecting to not have Mikey for his latest adventure. Jack sat in the car, feeling the skin between his teeth. He had bitten off her fingers, one by one, and he had bitten off her toes and her nipples and, finally, he had torn her throat open with his mouth and bathed in her flailing claret juices.

How beautiful it felt. How fresh and warm and nourishing. That's what it's all about. It's not about murder. It's about film and it's about life. The only way to live forever is on film. Nobody can take that away.

Jack wanted to write that down. He was suddenly seized by the idea of immortality. Perhaps vampirism could work after all. The way to stay immortal was through film, and the way to keep filming...was to keep killing.

Outside, waves crashed, the sun now lowering as if fat and desolate. Its light was no more than a simple glimmer of hope that was lost among the dead. As Jack exited the car, his maroon tie billowed in the warm breeze. He walked along the sand, DVD jewel case in his hand, and saw the tall, broad figure standing with his back turned toward him. Garretti no doubt. A sudden sensation of paranoia set in like a splinter. Jack felt as though he was being watched.

Jack whistled, and the mobster turned, both of them smiling beneath dark sunglasses. They approached each other with prudence. Garretti's hand came up first and Jack's followed. They greeted and shook.

"All done?" Garretti asked.

"Stick a fork in it," Jack said.

"Good. Oh, and we may need your services again."

"I don't do sequels," Jack said.

"How's Mikey?" Garretti asked.

Jack pulled his sunglasses from his face.

"You know," Jack said. "You keep asking me that, and I haven't heard from him in two days. Anything you feel like telling me?"

"No," Garretti held out a duffel bag with the rest of the cash in it.

Jack took it as the last of the day's light exited the sky.

"Have a good one." Jack tossed him the DVD.

Garretti turned and walked aimlessly along the sand, tucking the jewel case in his suit pocket. Jack watched him walk away and turned to leave.

A name for every bullet.

Part V:
Blood for Blood

Chapter Eighteen

Bill Corwin sat alone in his house.

A part of him had died long ago. A part of him was just being born. Marilyn committed suicide in a way he imagined only happened in Hollywood, and his daughter didn't deserve anything like what had happened to her. But sometimes in this sad, unfortunate world, what happens is for the best, even if it's death. Still, the unthinkable was allowed. This never would've happened if his brother, Ben, were still alive. Ben was also a novice filmmaker, they weren't this go—

What the hell do you mean not this good? The girl in the fucking videotape is—no, was—your daughter!

Yet, a part of him could imagine it was someone else, even though it would be police evidence soon enough. He had to get rid of the disc. There was no question about that. There was no stock option trade left in the world to get his wife back—or his daughter. That much he was certain of. His days of listening to her bullshit about borrowing the car and needing money, lying to them both, was over. Those days of walking along the boardwalk hand-in-hand sharing caramel popcorn and seeing a future vast beyond the depths of the ocean were also over.

A University of the Arts t-shirt...Jesus Christ.

They cut her fingers off... they used a coat hanger for...

"Enough!" Bill said aloud for his own benefit. Only the house remained. The police had already ruled Marilyn's death a suicide. His daughter would most likely be identified this evening. He heard they had fished something—someone—out of the canal.

God, please don't let it be her.

Although he had hated his daughter at times, he loved her too and still held out hope. It was a chilling feeling to realize that his love for her was the overriding emotion now.

What mattered most was moving on, if and when he ever could. It was doubtful and hardening to the heart to consider.

Chapter Nineteen

Jack had given up on Mikey, even as he banged on his door once more that morning, as the sun lifted along the California horizon. He felt nothing of interest.

The coffee in his car getting cold along with the bagels—an extra onion for Mikey just in case. Everything was growing stale with the oceanic wind. Jack walked down the street, paused and lit a cigarette. He dropped a few ashes against his t-shirt.

* * *

Fucking Mikey…where the fuck was this clown?

Bad choice of words. Let's try to forget about clowns for a while. I still have that bitch's skin stuck in my teeth. I can taste the perfume on it.

Jack smiled, crossed the street, and made it back to his car, somewhat surprised to find no messages on the cell phone that sat in the cup holder. No missed calls. In truth, he was waiting for Mikey to call him. The drive back, always the same. It's always a tethered ball tied to a pole, back and forth, back and forth. He decided against the morning wind and uprising sun that he'd quit the film business for a while. Well, he was lying to himself to some degree. He wouldn't quit, but just lay low for now.

There was a travel agent in Orange County he used to know pretty well. When he was still in the legit business, Wallace Jones got him free trips to Jamaica and sometimes the Galapagos Islands. It usually meant some free promo work or a timeshare pitch, but that was where Jack needed to be right now. He had plenty of money. No need to worry about that, especially if Mikey didn't turn up before he split.

What he *was* worried about was the front door of the townhouse sitting open when he pulled up. Darkness bloomed like a rose in a cellar. The dew glistening on the small patch of front yard made Jack's eyes squint as it caught the early morning sun.

"What the fuck?" Jack said. Suddenly he thought about Garretti and knew things had been much too good to be true. Garretti and his men had come for him. This was some type of set up for sure. Except, somehow, he knew that wasn't true either. They had no idea where he lived. Sure he could've been tracked, but for some reason Jack didn't believe that at all. The mob was on his side, at least the ones in LA. The guys in New York may think differently after watching his performance from two nights ago.

"Why is the front fucking door open?" Jack wondered why he had asked it out loud, peering for a moment at the door and then opening his glove box to reveal a Lugar. Nine shots and counting. He hoped he'd only need one.

The only person that knows about this place is Mikey.

Jack walked up to the stoop, never taking his eyes off the door. His cell phone shifted somewhere deep in his pocket. He wanted it to ring. He felt comfortable with the idea, but hated the revelation. He held the pistol in front of him, aimed at the front door. He only looked at it. The wind inched it open farther on an ancient creak. The sound reminded him of old movies about haunted houses, but the only thing haunted here was Jack.

"Who the fuck is in here?" Jack poked his head around the frame of the door.

Call the police…

"Stupid," Jack said, as if answering his own conscience.

He kicked the door all the way open.

Nothing.

He paused and leaned his head in, aiming the pistol outside.

"Who is in my fucking house?" his voice echoed. Again, only the small *pings* of the kitchen sink held the conversation in doubt. Jack decided he must've left the door open. That was all. No. That couldn't be right. It happens, but not when you're as careful as he had been.

The hallway lights came on with a flick of the switch, then the stairwell lights.

"Hello?"

Slowly, Jack ascended the staircase in front of him, the pistol aimed at all images of what would possibly zip around the corner any given minute with a knife in it's hand screaming obscenities and trying to kill him. Or worse, an axe. Or worse…a gun.

"Whoever is in my house, I'll fucking kill you without thinking twice. I never think twice. No sequels, asshole."

Jack reached the top of the stairs, rounded the corner and saw only his bedroom loft. The fan in the window was blowing with a steady hum. A blue balloon was tied to the grading of the fan, a souvenir of the games he had played with four foolish girls. The posters on the wall. Sid Vicious, Alistair Crowley, the lithograph painting mastered by the infamous serial killer John Wayne Gacy. The television on mute, showing Judge Judy. Pizza boxes crumpled with secret maggot-laden surprises writhing inside. Beer bottles lined up like soldiers, with others tumbled onto the old, carpeted floor. Photo albums with pictures of all his victims in them. His own painting of his foster mother, hanging in her damp, basement gallows, a very keen likeness. His CD collection, arranged in no particular order. His DVD collection—the most important thing.

Things had changed drastically from the well-organized world he left more than a year before, but nothing was different from how he had left it last night. He turned and strolled into the kitchen. The stained, molding puddle of spilled wine seeping from under the refrigerator, the smell of bleach and Listerine from the bathroom adjacent, was the same as he had left it. The crushed, used tampon with its horrid string still hanging over the lid of the toilet. An in-between pet project he had invited over to play riddles with, the ultimate riddle was when she announced during foreplay she was menstruating. He decided that was okay. She wanted to bleed; she got to bleed. Her baby blue dress was oh so lovely when he finished. The bathroom hadn't changed.

As his paranoia began to fade, Jack lowered his gun and laughed in the quietness of the kitchen. He saw the card table in the corner. The chainsaw resting on it, tendrils of flesh and blood and even teeth still stuck to the blade. Parts of a baby blue dress hung between the chains like ropes of flesh.

She had bled, indeed.

Nothing different here.

He saw from the corner, the alarm clock reading 12:00 and flashing. Jack looked at his watch. It was almost seven thirty. Sometime during the night, the power must've went out. No surprises there, considering the local track record of rolling blackouts. He had come back to sleep for a few hours and had simply not noticed. It was time to leave all this behind. Jack knew it. He would spend the rest of the morning packing his things for storage and getting the money together.

Walking into the living room, Jack saw a commercial on TV for a new horror flick he had no desire to see. It was nothing like real life, where the true horror films were made.

It's a way of becoming immortal…once you're on film, you never die…you live forever.

Jack grabbed the remote, lit another cigarette, and turned on Channel 8 Action News. The reporter was in the middle of telling a story about the police investigating what was shaping up to be a series of rapes and murders in the area. Jack only smiled, but when his eyes lowered to something sitting on the edge of the table the 42-inch monitor rested on, his smile turned into a curious frown.

Approaching it with caution, he saw a DVD jewel case. Across the case, a strap of duct tape. The kind he often used for his labeling. Written on the duct tape were two words written in thick black marker.

PLAY ME

What the fuck?

He slowly spun the DVD case in his hand and turned it around. He noticed droplets of dried blood on the case. Jack flipped it open, to the unlabeled disc inside. He was suddenly aware someone had been in the house since he left late last night.

PLAY ME

Jack carefully pulled the DVD free of the case and dropped it into the tray that opened at the touch of a button. The tray slid back inside, and the blue screen on the monitor suddenly went to a picture. The picture was fuzzy at first but cleared up almost instantly. He was looking at a man tied in a chair, naked. His chest was soaked in blood. A ski mask was pulled over his head. In his mouth, a leather ball gag, the ball itself bright yellow with a smiley face. There was a close up of the man's face; his terrified eyes under the mask were already lost in hopelessness. Jack sat down in his recliner, as he saw a man come into view, wearing jeans and no shirt. His mask was zippered and leather and shone under a swinging light to some desecrated brick-walled place. The man punched the guy in the chair once in the stomach, once in the face. The brass knuckles on his fist caught the light as well.

"You like that, bitch?" the torturer asked, his gut and chest sagging with the impact. He hit the man again, slammed him in the ribs, and this time, the victim pushed vomit out of the small gaps around the ball gag. Blood and yellow bile splattered the floor.

Amateur night, Jack thought. *But good enough...most definitely better than what was on television.*

Except he couldn't escape the reality in the mix of enjoyment.

Who knows about our projects? Why show me this?

But there were plenty of people; the Brotello gang, Garretti's crew, the customers who placed orders. It wasn't exactly a secret anymore in certain circles.

Jack saw the torturer reveal a knife that would make Rambo jealous. Its left side serrated, its right side reflecting. The masked filmmaker turned toward the camera.

"Watch this" he barked and turned and plunged the knife through his victim's right kneecap, twisting the bone with one splintering crack. The man in the chair shit himself almost immediately. The pain obviously severe and intolerable. The man vomited again, and continued to vomit. When the torturer took a straight razor and held it to his victim's right wrist, he screamed in his ear.

"Was it fun for you, you fucking murderer? You fucking shit bag." He slit the victim's right wrist and used his own thumb to pull out an artery. Blood erupted in streams; ropes of it snaked all over the victim's left leg. He repeated with the left wrist.

"And now for the main event." The torturer was playing to the camera again, more for Jack than for himself. He grabbed the victim's mask and pulled it off, revealing the prize. Jack's cigarette fell from his lips.

He knew where Mikey had been.

"I thought you'd like to look into his eyes before I do it.... Just like he looked into my daughter's...blood for blood...is that fair? I don't know, John. You tell me. You think it's fair my wife cut her goddamn wrists?"

Jack looked on, horrified, amazed, and aroused all at once.

"I think it's fair...hell...I think it's *perfect.*"

The masked torturer took a wine bottle and drank it down to all the demons floating at the bottom before breaking off the neck. Pieces of dark glass flew around the room, and the masked man grabbed Mikey by his bare cock while he screamed into the ball gag, a gag that was not a ball at all but merely a painted grenade.

"After all the movies you made...here's the award winner."

The torturer began to twist the jagged shards of the wine bottle onto Mikey's crotch, the sharp broken ends pushing into his flesh and ripping at what was left of his manhood. He would fuck no more. His days of raping were over. He was screaming for help. He was screaming to be let free. He was screaming for Jack.

The wine bottle tore open his plumbing, but the worst came when the masked man pulled the pin on the grenade stuffed in Mikey's mouth and backed away behind the video camera. He uttered words that would haunt Jack Sanders forever.

"My wife lost her mind in the bathtub...now we'll watch him lose his."

Jack rushed to turn the film off, but it was too late. The grenade went off. He did make it to the switch finally, and once the button was pressed, the set went dead. He stood, breathing heavily in the center of the room.

"What the fuck is this?" he asked, but silence was the only response, the room now empty and his thoughts trailing back to the images he had just seen.

Only a moment passed before Jack Sanders took his foot and smashed the television set in a rage. Grabbing the mirrored tray he and Mikey had chopped rails on so many late nights and early mornings, he tossed it across the room. Outside, the light was getting hotter and cars had started to pass on the street.

As pathetic as it sounded, Mikey had been the closest thing Jack Sanders ever had to family, and he felt the closest thing he had ever felt to true pain.

You fucked up, Jack… you killed Bill Corwin's daughter…

He would have said sorry, but it was too late for apologies, and when Corwin pulled that pin, revenge quickly replaced any faux concern he might have mustered.

Jack walked across the living room, past the staircase and into the kitchen. He looked around for his Lugar. He wasn't sure what he was going to do, but he had a few ideas brewing. When he came back across the staircase to the living room, he realized he had left the bullets behind. He went across the staircase again, and this time, when he came back, someone was standing right behind him.

* * *

Outside, in the early morning light, a town car pulled to the side of the road and halted at the sidewalk. A few seconds later, the driver emerged, smiling, wearing sunglasses and strong cologne. It was business as usual for Garretti. As he approached the front of the house, he hoped to find Jack. When he heard glasses breaking and dishes being smashed, he knew he was in the right place.

* * *

"Recognize the face, motherfucker?" the man behind Jack asked. It was Bill Corwin, wearing Mikey's latex George Bush mask. Jack didn't answer, just looked on in disgust. Ignoring the 9mm aimed at his face.

"You checked everything but your closet."

"I guess I won't make that mistake again." Jack smirked.

"No…I guess not. I shot all your dogs, and I made Mikey show me everything. I saw all the places you've been."

Jack held up his middle finger. "Did you see *this* place?"

"I'm going to put a bullet right between your nuts motherfucker, then we'll see how fucking spunky you are, John."

You're still calling me John. I guess Mikey didn't tell you everything, huh?

"Bill…" Jack said, "it's not our fault we picked your actual daughter for the film."

Jack felt the butt of Bill's gun break his nose in two separate places and sprawled backward across the floor. Pushing himself back, he grabbed the Lugar off the couch. Still no bullets, but Bill didn't know it and took a step back, now on both sides of a weapon.

"You're about to join your white trash friend," Bill spat, obviously beginning to realize he was in over his head but keeping up the act anyway. "I hope you liked my movie. I can be creative, too, you know. My wife was when she slit her goddamn wrists."

"Married to you I can see why." Jack smiled, as Bill pulled the mask free.

Jack used the moment to grab a spilled beer bottle and hurled it at Bill's face. It was half full when it shattered across the bridge of his nose, sending emerald glass around the room. Bill's hands instinctively went up to his nose, and Jack rushed out of the room and into the kitchen. He went for one thing, and it wasn't the bullets.

Running after Jack in a rage, Bill Corwin was all but temporarily blinded by beer and broken glass, but even with only partial vision he saw the chainsaw being swiped from the kitchen table. Jack didn't have time to start it, but there was enough time to swing it full force across the remains of Bill's face.

Before he could maneuver the swing, however, Bill fired two rounds at point blank range, one hitting the blade of the saw—making Jack drop it—and the other splitting off wildly into the ceiling. Jack charged before he could get another round off and landed a knee in his face. Bill went down with his stomach lurching, but managed to grab a paring knife and ram it through the top of Jack's left boot. It didn't go all the way through, but deep enough to make him stagger. He screamed and kicked Bill in the face with his good foot until his nose was nothing more than bone marbles stuffed in fleshy sausage meat.

Bill managed to get another shot off, this time grazing Jack's left cheek. A small, thin rope of blood jetted outward and upward. Jack wasted no time diving on Bill and trying to wrestle the gun away, but it went off again, hitting the front door dead center. What neither of them knew at that moment was the bullet had gone through the door and into Garretti's chest.

Garretti had tracked him down to offer Jack breakfast and a new job, but when the bullet split between his ribs, those offers were revoked. The mobster backed up, his feet shaking and knees buckling. His fists hammering together as his whole body began to shake. He tried to keep from falling, the look on his face more surprise than anger. But he ended up in the dead bushes next to the porch steps as Jack and Bill came crashing through the door just seconds after the bullet. Jack was the first one up and registered Garretti only enough to jump over his body. He didn't stop, not even with the knowledge that somehow he would be blamed for that killing as well. Instead, Jack jumped in the GTO as a bloody-faced Bill Corwin charged out behind him and tripped over Garretti's body.

As Jack fumbled for the keys, an impending feeling of doom starting to linger,

Bill ran toward the car, firing the rest of the clip into the driver's side. The first thing to go was the window.

shattering into thousands of shards. Another bullet slammed into the door just as Jack's hand came up with the keys. Watching him pull away, Bill headed for the motorcycle he had stashed behind the house, but Garretti grabbed him first.

"Who the fuck are you, asshole?" Bill asked.

"Mikey…" Garretti answered, choking on the blood that had managed to make its way up from his guts.

"Mikey? Mikey's *dead*," Bill fired a bullet into Garretti's head, rewetting the morning grass.

Chapter Twenty

The pizza shop on 45th was where the police dispatch was called in. During the early morning hours, it opened for breakfast. Bagels and runny eggs mostly, the kind Jack enjoyed the most. He had a thing for bagels almost as much as Bill Corwin had a thing for bullets, but even moving at ninety miles an hour now, Jack knew that Bill's real problem wasn't Mikey or the film or even that his daughter was brutally tortured and killed. No, Bill Corwin's problem was that he *liked* it.

Dough Boy's Pizza had opened thirty minutes earlier, and the first customer of the day, Emma Stoltsfus, was just walking out as the GTO rounded the corner. Seventy-five years on this earth, Emma had spent the last ten of those hooked to a colostomy bag with cataracts that seemed to crust over more and more each day. She stepped off the sidewalk with her cane as the tires on the GTO let out a squeal. The man inside the car was wiping blood out of his eyes. It was all over his white t-shirt featuring the likeness of Jim Morrison.

People are strange. Really fucking strange.

Not far behind him came Bill Corwin, racing at top speed on a crotch rocket that he looked ridiculously old on.

Emma never saw it coming, but the fry cook, the one Jack always insisted make his bagels—because he understood the proper cream cheese ratio—came out screaming at the top of his lungs. He let out something that resembled "Watch out!"

Emma turned her head slightly to the left, while standing in the middle of the road, almost as if she could hear her death coming and welcomed it. In any case, she never saw the car until the grill was less than ten yards away. The GTO hit her at seventy miles an hour. Her cane turning into a weather vane, that's where it ended up, on the roof of the second-floor apartment above the nail parlor next door. She was dead on impact, but that didn't make it any easier to take. She was propelled so high in the air she actually reached the height of the telephone poles and came back down with both hips broken and her life spewing from every orifice, her colostomy bag tangled up in Jack's windshield wipers.

When Emma hit the ground, it forced all the teeth in her mouth, including her fixed dentures, to blow out the middle of her face. Pieces of bridgework turned into shrapnel, zipping across the air like bullets. If she were alive, she would have been able to taste her own shit. Her body was still shaking violently as Jack laughed and thought about how funny it was that people still had reflex capabilities after death.

He hoped her body would cause Bill to fall off his bike, but Bill's reflexes were as fast as Emma's dying ones, and he maneuvered with the grace of Evil Kenevel out of the way and around Emma's still-convulsing body. By now, a crowd had started to gather, staring at Emma's brains, which had splattered cars on both sides of the sidewalk.

Jack raced onward, as behind him Bill Corwin fired round after round at the speeding car trying to target the back of Jack's head. When Jack made it onto the highway, the chase briefly picked up speed, before he swung the GTO off at the first exit. They ended up on the outskirts of Lunag Woods, driving alone under the morning sun, with evergreens surrounding both sides. Jack pushed the speedometer up toward ninety miles an hour and decided on a plan.

What happened next was as close to a miracle as Jack would ever see. Bill's pursuit led them past a state police car parked behind an embankment, adding a third vehicle to the chase. For Bill Corwin, who had given up hope of making it out alive, it was of no importance. He would do whatever it took to bring John down, even if it meant an expedited trip to hell, and he pushed the front tire of the bike just feet from the ass-end of the GTO.

The brake lights flashed blood red, and Bill swerved left, dumping the bike and sliding across a hundred and fifty feet of gravel and, now, skin. Jack spun out of control, the car going full circle. He managed something that resembled traction in the middle of the road, looking back at the spilled bike and what he hoped was a dead Bill Corwin. The cop car screeched behind him.

"That's right, motherfucker!" Jack laughed from the shot-out rear window. "You tell Satan I said he…"

But before he finished, a tractor trailer truck barreled across the intersection, clipping the front end of the GTO and sending it spinning again, this time into a tax ditch full of briars and bushes. After contact, the tractor-trailer careened into a nearby tree, causing the driver to make an unexpected exit through the windshield with such force that most of his jaw and right arm were left behind. He ended up plastered against the splintered trunk of the tree, his last thoughts of his family now smeared across the bark.

* * *

Forever seemed almost like yesterday, but it came quickly for Jack, who woke with more pain than he could remember ever feeling. His vision was blurred as he sat up in the car, seeing smoke billowing from the crumpled hood. His eyes refused to focus, but he realized rather quickly something was wrong. He heard a gunshot. But it was different from the sound that had followed him across the city. This sounded much larger.

It's over now…Jack thought as he crawled out of the car and onto his belly. He hesitated to relax his aching body, still feeling as shattered as the car. His nose was fractured and so was his leg. Compared to Bill, though, his injuries were minor.

As Jack collapsed among the buzzing of bees, he noticed a single flower that had somehow missed the car as it came to rest in the ditch. He knew more cops would come. Why the cop that was chasing him hadn't come over yet remained a mystery. Jack forced himself to crawl and finally emerged at the edge of the right-of-way. He had no weapons and hoped he was the only one left alive. All he could see in the distance was the decimated California Highway Patrol car, sitting in the middle of what was now an otherwise deserted road. The lights on top of the cruiser were still flashing and the windshield looked like it was smashed in with blood and glass. In reality, the safety glass had blown outward, and inside the patrol car, Jack saw the cop. He was half slumped back in the seat, his neck bent sideways at an acute angle. His eyes were wide, and a blue fly had parked itself on the left one, crawling around tentatively waiting for a blink. That wasn't going to happen, though. The gaping hole in the center of his chest made that clear.

When Jack looked down at his belt, he noticed that the officer's gun was gone. Another quick glance, and he saw there was a shotgun locked against the dashboard in an upright position. Looking around, Jack still heard a buzzing. Wherever Bill had run off to, it had been quick. Except Jack knew he couldn't be in any condition to travel. When he found the right key on the dead cop's gun belt and unhinged the shotgun from the dash, a new group of sounds emerged from the south.

More cops are coming...

Jack hurried around the cruiser and saw the motorcycle lying on its side. When he turned to his right, he saw Bill Corwin emerge from the woods, pulling up his zipper, the other hand still on the cop's pistol.

"Had to take a piss. Figured I'd get it out of the way before I killed you." Bill smiled. "I couldn't help it. Although if I'd known I was going to piss blood, I probably would've waited until you *were* dead."

Bill spat, blood erupting from his lips. The left side of his body and face were littered with gravel and dirt from the street. His helmet had saved him from certain death, but his jeans were ripped down the side and his left arm was bleeding around a compound fracture that had exposed the bone just above his wrist. Still, he moved toward Jack, dragging his leg behind him like a zombie. Jack had played the occasional zombie in films for Horace Deerling, and he had played dead men as well. If one of those bullets came any closer to Jack's head, he wouldn't have to worry about acting.

"Fuck you." It was Jack's turn to smile. He swung around, the shotgun's massive barrel now eye level with Bill Corwin, who ducked back into the bushes as the first shot went off, echoing through the trees like a trumpet from hell. It missed Bill, and he returned fire. One, two, three shots, before a new and final clip clicked tight.

Taking advantage of Bill's limp and efforts to reload, Jack took off, heading across a sparsely planted field toward a cluster of buildings that looked like the remains of a manufacturing district outside of town. He made his way through the thin shrubbery and to the shell of a deserted factory that had been out of commission for years. Glancing back only once, Bill attempted to hobble after him. The sound of sirens was much clearer.

The building was in shambles, half broken and falling over, desecrated and obviously nothing more now than a spot where teenagers could get drunk and fuck. Jack made it into the front of the building, while Bill pressed on.

Jack stood on the other side of the dark chambers that were buried in dust, dried rat shit, and dead cockroaches. When he heard Bill slide open the industrial doors, he pumped the shotgun as quietly as he could.

"I'm coming for you, bitch!" Bill screamed. "I'm going to send you to be with Jenny and Marilyn. You're going to see what hell is like. You're getting two bullets, one for each of them. You're going—"

But before he could finish, Jack stepped out into the open entrance of the factory and pulled the trigger on the dead cop's shotgun. The sound was enormous, almost pre-historic, and Bill's face lit up in surprise as his right ear disappeared, his shock quickly turning to pain. He dropped down behind an old rusty grave of heavy machine parts, managing to hang on to his gun.

"My ear! You motherfucker. That was my ear!"

Bill's right hand moved up to the place where his ear once was, but found only a smear of dark blood and torn cartilage. A ringing that was actually closer to the absence of sound flooded his mind. A tag of skin that was once his right earlobe still hung on.

"I'm warning you," Jack said calmly. "Back off now. I got three shots left, and they're all marked for another part of your face. You come out from behind that shit pile and guess what I'll shoot off next? But hey, after seeing your daughter get fucked, it probably won't matter anyhow."

Silence was the only response, then a bird, a vulture, flying high above the patchwork roof in the early afternoon sky. Jack receded back into the darkness of the adjoining room, snaking his way past old machinery and rusted-out oil barrels.

He waited, watching for what seemed like the better part of fifteen minutes. Finally, Bill broke the silence, his voice slicing through the shadows of the factory.

"Ready to die?" Bill asked without much real interest in a response. He was hidden in the same shadows he had disrupted, but Jack slowly slid the shotgun barrel out above the top of a wooden beam, hoping for the best.

"You took everything from me—Marilyn, Jenny, my fucking *ear*!"

I know a good plastic surgeon for that; they have lots of magicians in Hollywood. You should've seen what I looked like before I went under the knife, Jack almost answered.

"You can't beat me," Bill said. "I've got more rounds than you."

"I only need one, asshole," Jack answered, making Bill's shadow turn in his direction. Jack Sanders realized it had all come down to this, to one bad customer, to one extreme bloodletting. He and Mikey had made a terrible mistake, and they had finally come to their last hurrah. The curtain had fallen.

"You're not getting away with what you did to Mikey. You hear me?" Jack asked. "I'm not going to let that happen."

"Oh, I hear you, but you're as good as dead anyway. Ironic isn't it?"

"What's that?"

"Don't you recognize this place from Mikey's last performance? His blood is still on the walls of the old offices above you. What are the fucking odds?"

Jack came out from hiding, just as a blade of light found Bill's shoulder. It was enough. Four shots became three, but Bill disappeared into the thick, dusty dark of the farthest corner.

"I learned this in the business, Bill!" Jack screamed. "Everything in your life is nothing more than an audition! Film is immortality Can you grasp that? I am fucking *forever!*"

Jack entered the half lit hallway, following the droplets of fresh blood. The trail would lead to Bill Corwin.

"That's the pay off...the real curtain call."

Jack spun toward the edge of the darkness, fired off another shot, then another. Birds nesting above scattered. One shot left. Jack loaded his final shot and pumped. It was going to go between the eyes of Bill Corwin's bloodied face. He was going to look into those eyes and wait for him to beg, then answer with the pull of the trigger. Jack took two steps forward and saw something large to his left. He smiled, knowing what it was. Bill thought he was covered by the dark, but Jack saw him.

"Oh, Billy..." Jack said. "I guess this is our predictable climax."

Out of the dark came a hand flashing the chrome of the highway patrolman's service weapon, the barrel pressing firmly against Jack Sander's throbbing temple. Bill's voice came from behind it.

"No, John. This is the end."

Jack's eyes closed. The figure he thought was Bill was the body of Mikey. Propped against the wall, it became clear as his eyes further adjusted. The hammer of the gun clicked back.

Darkness.

Part VI:
Closure

Chapter Twenty-One

The sun was creeping below the horizon, casting elongated shadows across the driveway as Susan Grier pulled off of the quiet suburban street and into the driveway of the house her family had called home since their daughter was born almost two decades ago.

Her husband's sedan wasn't in the garage as she stepped from the SUV and headed toward the mailbox, but that wasn't unusual these days. Ever since their daughter Heather had gone missing, Susan and Rick Grier had been working later, running pointless errands and doing whatever it took to avoid one another. Their relationship had been less than perfect before Heather's disappearance, and with her gone, there was nothing left but a shell of a marriage. Before, they had stayed together for Heather; now, they stayed together because both were afraid of losing the last remaining connection to their daughter.

Susan flipped through the day's mail, trying not to let herself get her hopes up for a letter from Heather, a ransom note, anything that meant she wasn't lost forever.

But for the 412th day since Heather had went missing from her job at the animal shelter, the United States Post Office failed to deliver hope. Bills, credit applications, mass mailers, but nothing from Heather.

Officially, the case was still open, and the common thought was that Heather was more than likely the victim of whatever killing spree had turned up the dismembered bodies of young women throughout southern California in recent months, but the calls from the police were less frequent now and the journalists had all but forgotten about Heather's disappearance. For all intents and purposes, life was back to normal in the Grier's sleepy neighborhood, but for Susan, the pain and helplessness were as intense as ever. They may have forgotten, but she hadn't.

Susan was leafing through the junk mail, dropping the unwanted envelopes into an outside trash can, still damp with rain water, when she noticed a package on the front doorstep. She had ordered a pair of Uggs (Heather would have disapproved of the calf skin) a week or so ago, but this box was much too small to be boots. With the exception of the Grier's handwritten address, the box was void of any markings. No labels, no return address.

After kicking off her shoes just inside the front door, Susan Grier tossed the package onto the coffee table and forgot about it while she poured herself a gin and tonic and grabbed three Percocets from a drawer in the kitchen—two more bad habits she'd picked up since Heather vanished. By the time she had changed into sweats, her first drink of the afternoon was all but gone and the pills had helped a much-needed numbness set in. Only after she poured herself another gin did she remember the box and make her way over to the couch.

Inside the box was a clear-plastic DVD case. In black, box lettering, someone had written "CLOSURE" across the disc contained in the case. There was no insert or letter with the DVD, and by the time she turned on the television, Susan's pulse had managed to push its way through the Percocet stupor.

* * *

When Rick Grier walked through the front door, his wife of 24 years was slumped on the couch, staring blankly at the blue default screen of the DVD player. The ice in her drink had melted and condensation from the glass had formed in a small puddle on the coffee table. The door closed behind him with a loud click but didn't snap Susan from her daze.

"Honey?"

There was no response—no acknowledgment that she was even aware of his presence as he walked across the living room and stood beside the couch.

"What's the matter?" He glanced at the "DVD" logo bouncing around the television screen.

Susan didn't answer her husband. Instead, she simply picked up the remote and pressed play, starting from the beginning what had played over-and-over in her mind since she first watched it more than hour ago.

The screen went to black for a full fifteen seconds before snapping to a wide shot of what looked like a rotted-out manufacturing warehouse of some sort. In the center of the screen was a man, stripped naked and tied to a steel support beam, his arms stretched out above his head and his ankles bound to the ends of a three-foot length of scrap metal, forcing him to stand with his legs spread shoulder width apart.

"What the hell is this?" Rick asked his wife.

"I don't know," were the first words out of Susan's mouth since he had walked through the door.

"Does this have something to do with Heather." The optimism in his voice was not hidden well at all.

"I'm not sure."

"Well where the fuck did..." Rick Grier was stopped mid-question by movement on the screen.

A second man entered the frame and began carefully examining objects resting on a spread out sheet beside the bound man, before finally settling on what looked to Rick like a small paring knife.

"Is this real?"

"I think so." Susan had wondered the same thing the first time she watched the DVD.

The bound man's head hung down, exposing his mildly receding hairline, but jerked up when the dulled blade touched the flesh of his chest. The second man—the apparent filmmaker—started carving; etching names into his victim's skin. Just below his collar bone "Jennifer." Below that "Marilyn." And so on. After a dozen or so more names, the list ended just above the man's pelvis. The last name Rick Grier saw sliced into the man's abdomen was a familiar one. "Heather."

When he was finished carving, the filmmaker lifted the head of his victim for the camera. Full of pain, but nothing that resembled surprise, it was a face that was unfamiliar to the Griers but one they wouldn't ever forget.

It was the face of Jack Sanders.

Chapter Twenty-Two

For Bill Corwin, killing Mikey and John hadn't given him the closure he had hoped for, but at least there wouldn't be any more victims.

And who knows what it might mean for their families?

After securing John—and a short visit to the hospital—he had returned to the warehouse off of Exit 1 with a video camera and his "tools." He hadn't been home and the cops had yet to track him down, but with the registration on his trashed bike at the crash scene, Bill knew it was only a matter of time.

When he was done with John, he had returned to the townhouse, making sure to push the body of Garretti behind the limited shrubbery on his way in. In their makeshift studio, he'd found the editing suite and did his best to cut together the footage he'd shot and burn it onto a disc. With his limited knowledge of the software, the process had taken him nearly four hours and looked amateur at best. But at that moment, the lack of transitions or a soundtrack were the last things on Bill Corwin's mind.

Comparing the contents of John's hard drive with the missing persons reports online and on television, identifying the victims hadn't been hard, and he had located the families of more than half of them. Some of the victims had not shown up as missing, however.

Probably whores. I can't be responsible for everything.

Bill immediately regretted thinking that way about the girls in the films he had forced himself to watch for several hours after he was finished editing his project. As disheveled as their living and work space had been, the men were careful not to leave a paper trail of any sort, and the work was as tedious as it was sickening.

Now, with his work complete and the names of the victims he could identify in his pocket, Bill made his way to the stairs leading from John and Mikey's twisted work space, dumping gas from a bright red can behind him as he went. When he reached the top of the steps, he lit his Zippo and tossed it onto the trail of gasoline.

By the time he got to the end of the street in his car, he could already see flames through the first floor windows.

Chapter Twenty-Three

Bishop Kincaid hadn't known Father Bedard, but he'd heard the stories.

He came to St. Michael Parish about two months after Bedard's disappearance. His second week at the parish, they had discovered the body, or what remained of it anyhow.

Whispered rumors made their way through the church, just like any other place of business, becoming fodder for the imaginations of the oppressed priests and parishioners. The medical examiner had discovered what appeared to be more than eighty-five nail-sized holes in Bedard's skin and flesh. The damage done to his wrists and feet was far worse and led to speculation of stigmata.

The more cynical of the parishioners knew better. The extremely cynical didn't have to think too long to make assumptions about what the assault may have been retaliation for.

Either way, Bishop Kincaid had put it out of his mind—something his predecessor had been unable to do before his departure—until he had come back from a hospital visit that afternoon to find an unmarked DVD with the day's stack of mail.

There was no return address, and Kincaid assumed it was a copy of a new faith-based commercial venture. Piles of similar promotional materials had formed in his office since he first took over nearly four months ago, but that assumption quickly vanished after he stopped off in the confirmation classroom an hour or so later to view the disc on the church's only DVD player.

There wasn't a word for the level of shock Kincaid felt after pressing play. Nothing he had heard during confessionals or read in the book of Revelations during his fifty-seven years of life had prepared him for this.

In the flickering light of the out-dated television set, Kincaid watched as the man's chest was carved with names—including that of Father Bedard. From there, the second man on screen took his time breaking each of his victim's fingers; all while letting him, "John," know this was his fault. As he cut out John's tongue, he also made reference to someone named Mikey.

By the time the torturer told John he was leaving his eyes in so he "could see the rest of what he had coming," the blood from the man's mouth had rendered the names on his chest illegible.

Bishop Kincaid clicked the mute button at that point, sitting—stunned—for several minutes before collecting himself, slowly reaching for the phone, and dialing the police.

As he waited to be connected to an unnamed detective, the images continued to flash on the screen behind him. The torturer's screaming came out between silent fits of anger. The victim appeared to be beyond the point of screaming.

But appearances were deceiving. In reality, Jack Sanders had howled as Bill Corwin sodomized him with his own hunting knife, parts of his colon and lower intestines falling out behind him with every withdraw of the blade.

Chapter Twenty-Four

Bill coasted slowly down the street he had called home for the past eight years. The Corwins had moved in six months after his big promotion, and the house served them well through Jenny's teenage years. But now, as he kept an eye out for any sign of the police, it all seemed like a waste.

Easing to a stop two blocks from his home at the end of the cul-de-sac, Bill still hadn't spotted any activity.

Maybe enough of the bike had been destroyed.

Bill only allowed the optimism for a moment. The cops hadn't pieced it together yet, but there was no way he was that lucky. Still, until they showed up he was determined to make the most of his freedom, and he made his way to the back of the house, trying to draw as little attention as possible from any would be onlookers.

Acting on instinct, Bill walked into the kitchen first, pressing play on the answering machine before making his way to the refrigerator.

"Marilyn, this is Howie at Fitness World. You missed your training session today…"

She's losing weight a different way now. No workout needed.

Bill opened the refrigerator door, the stink of rotting tuna salad and pomegranates smacking him in the back of the throat.

"Bill, Ted here. Hadn't heard from you today, and no one has seen you around the office. Call me as soon as you get this to talk about the Davidson reports. The deadline is coming up, and we need to make sure everything is in order…"

We? Not a fucking chance, Teddy boy.

Still reeling from the stench, Bill slammed the refrigerator door and stepped back, grasping at composure.

"This message is for Bill Corwin. This is detective Jim Young with the California Highway Patrol. A motorcycle with partial plates, matching the description of a vehicle registered in your name, was recovered from the site of an accident yesterday morning. Please return this call at your earliest convenience so we can straighten all this out…"

Well, so much for being public enemy number one.

Confident he had some time—the message from Detective Young was only three hours old—Bill made his way upstairs to the office that had served as his daily den of vice until five days ago. Behind him, Ted's voice trailed off in a second message.

* * *

Bill worked methodically throughout the afternoon, copying his second and final film to DVDs and addressing them to the families of John and Mikey's victims.

The guilt balling up in his gut had nothing to with killing the men who had raped and tortured his daughter. Instead, there was a creeping feeling of understanding. When he had cleaned pieces of Mikey's skull from his hair he felt righteous; when he twisted the hunting knife into John's ass he had enjoyed himself. More and more, the line between socially acceptable perversion and the person Bill Corwin had become in the past several days blurred in his mind. He and John weren't so different, and the thought scared the hell out of him.

Between labeling and addressing the DVDs, pictures of Marilyn and Jenny haunted Bill.

His wife's blood mixing with the lukewarm bath water and staining the white porcelain of the tub.

Bill knew it was his fault.

The barbwire-wrapped coat hanger tearing up Jenny. His idea of perverse revenge destroying his daughter's womb.

The come on his hands and keyboard had matched the seminal fluid and blood mixture coating his only child's young face. He had paid for this. He had gotten off watching it. Would he have been able to stop mid-stroke if he'd known it was her?

He knew the answer was no, and the shame made Bill's hand shake as he scribbled "CLOSURE" on the final DVD before packing it in an unmarked box.

Chapter Twenty-Five

When Marcus Brotello played the "CLOSURE" DVD that arrived in that day's mail, what filled the flat screen hanging on the wall in his study surprised him. It wasn't the violent content—the man's face was twisted in pain but looked vaguely familiar as he writhed and bled— but rather the players involved with the film.

He had contracted a man to make a similar, although more theatrical, film months before, and when his niece Desmond had gone missing a few weeks ago, he suspected retribution from Garretti and his boys. There had been bad blood between the crews in the decade that had passed since the robbery. His sister had cried almost non-stop since Desmond never came home from the clubs, and Brotello knew it wasn't a coincidence. Garretti must have pieced together the puzzle surrounding the experiment in brutality he contracted with some of his rival's girls. When the DVD arrived that afternoon, he was certain he knew what awaited him and was already thinking of ways to break the news to his sister. It was hard to call a man with the handle of a hunting knife protruding from his ass a pleasant surprise, but in the life Brotello had created for himself, you thanked God for small favors.

On screen, the man, who Brotello was certain he had met before, had gone silent. His destroyed body had finally given out and his torturer seemed pleased with himself as the picture faded out.

From downstairs, Brotello could hear his sister sobbing again, asking the housekeeper "Why?" over and over.

Brotello knew why, but allowed himself to smile, knowing he had at least one more day until he'd have to break the news.

Either way, Garretti would pay.

Unfortunately for Brotello's sense of poetic justice, Garretti's decomposing body had been consumed by a house fire three days prior. No one had seemed to notice; the lessee was nowhere to be found and the investigation had been brief and superficial at best. As far as the fire marshal was concerned, it was just another case of faulty wiring and bad luck.

Chapter Twenty-Six

For Bill Corwin, the days since he returned home had passed uneventfully.

Ted had stopped calling and a return call to Detective Young had resolved any questions about his involvement in the crash. The bike had been stolen, he told Young, who seemed eager enough to believe Bill's story and let it go at that. The police would be forwarding the report to him for insurance purposes.

"It should be there within six weeks," Young had informed him.

Bill doubted he'd be around long enough to deal with the paperwork. His days were filled with nothing but grief and memories of Marilyn and Jenny. What had happened haunted him.

Blood and come. Come and blood.

In Bill's mind, the two were now inseparable.

His DVDs had made the news, and the police were starting to piece everything together. Some of the families interviewed on camera seemed relieved, glad to put everything behind them, but for Bill, closure remained an unattainable dream.

He wandered the house, taking in the rooms—some of them dingy, paths worn into the carpets, others barely lived in. The Corwins' house had ceased being a home, and Bill realized the extent of the solitude he and his wife had lived in. A week had passed since Marilyn's death and no one but him seemed to notice. The other victims' families had seen this horrid chapter come to a close, but who was here to witness the end for Marilyn and Jenny?

The only other person with a true connection to Bill and Marilyn had been gone since birth. Their son had become nothing more than the ghost of a memory in the years since. Adopted by a family in Pennsylvania, the

Corwins had never broached the subject, but now, Bill suddenly needed him with an almost unexplainable desperation. He needed Marilyn to be remembered, and their son—he didn't even know his name—was Bill's only hope.

It was a last, and probably despondent, attempt at closure, but Bill Corwin had nothing left to lose.

In fact, he had nothing left at all.

* * *

Adoption information was officially confidential, and Bill was surprised at how easily he was able to dig up the details from a child born more than three decades before. A call to a family friend that worked with the state's department of social services, a few favors called in, and a promise of anonymity, and all he needed to know was e-mailed to him in less than a day.

The irony wasn't lost on Bill. As he sat on the bed he had shared with Marilyn, he realized that at any point he could have made contact with his son, but only when he had lost everything else did he take the necessary steps. With no family left, he wanted something to hold on to—something new to destroy.

He found his answer in the form of an e-mail attachment.

All the other DVDs had been turned over the U.S. Postal Service with no explanation; the recipients able to piece together what they needed to know of the story from the disappearance of their loved ones. For his estranged son, however, Bill included a three-page, hand-written letter outlining his sins—the original film, Marilyn and Jenny's death, his retribution. He held nothing back, baring his soul and deepest secrets to a son he had abandoned thirty-seven years prior.

The boy—no, he would be a man now—had grown up without his biological parents, had been subjected to horrors Bill would never understand, and now, he would be forced into the role of absolver and heir to an unknown father's mortal mistakes.

Bill should have felt guilt, but he was beyond that now. As he signed off at the bottom of the letter, he felt as close to calm as he had in years.

His crimes were no longer his.

Chapter Twenty-Seven

A gun didn't seem ceremonious enough, and after Marilyn, opening his wrists was out of the question.

It had taken Bill longer to choose the appropriate method of suicide than it had to make the decision to go ahead with it. There was nothing left for him in this world, and killing John and Mikey had given him a sense of finality, if not closure.

With a 10-inch loop laid out, the end of the rope was then wound around itself four times before being carefully laced back through.

If Bill was at peace with the decision, however, his shaking hands betrayed him as he made his final preparations. The last package and his confession letter had been addressed to his son and placed by the Corwin's mailbox for pickup. His life insurance and will now named the son he hadn't seen since he was born as the sole beneficiary and heir. In death he figured to be a better father than he had in life.

The Scaffold—or Gallows—Knot is based on the Multifold Overhand Knot. The history associated with its name was hard to miss.

Like every day prior to his involvement with the whole sordid mess that claimed his wife and daughter, Bill woke at five forty-five, made coffee and showered before taking out the length of braided, white nylon rope and placing it on the desk beside his best suit and the tie Jenny had given him two Christmases ago. Ironically, it was also the first morning since witnessing her death Bill had the desire to jerk off, but that would have to wait.

A Gallows Knot is also used to attach fishing line to angling-rods.

Bill found a stud in the ceiling and attached the heavy-duty chandelier bracket he had picked up the afternoon before. After taking his time with the knot, he

172

threaded the tail of rope through the bracket and secured it. He tested his weight by swinging on it. Satisfied with the apparatus, he dressed, leaving the double Windsor of the tie loose around his neck to make room for the second knot. The arrangements finished, he stood on a desk chair in the center of the office and distractedly ran his index finger around the inside of the nylon loop.

His finger stopped when it reached the noose. Something wasn't right.

Climbing down from the swiveling chair—probably not the best idea in retrospect—he made his way over to the computer and opened the media player. At the bottom of the display screen it still showed the name of the last file played—"cvdrip.ar_studentsnuff.wav"—but Bill didn't notice as he switched over to the media library and chose the last song he would ever hear.

With the small distance between the ceiling and the noose, strangulation would be the cause of death—what was known as a "short drop" hanging.

Fifty-four years in the world, more than five decades of pop music had come and gone in Bill Corwin's life, and in the end he settled on The Beatles' "I Want to Hold Your Hand."

Back on the chair, trying his best not to twist before he shouted, Bill was as ready as he was going to get and slipped the noose over his head, slowly tightening the knot just below his Adam's apple. He took a deep breath and slid the chair out from under his best pair of dress shoes in one awkward sweep. His body jerked against the weight of itself and his cock got harder than it had had been since he was 17-years-old. The release he denied himself earlier that morning came out in sticky globs, mixing between his legs with the shit that now ran down his thighs.

If he believed in an afterlife, he would have looked forward to reuniting with his wife and daughter. As it was, hypoxia assured the only person Bill Corwin would be making a connection with was the coroner.

Beneath his dangling feet the remnants of the last of his natural bodily functions formed in a rank puddle.

Chapter Twenty-Eight

He was more than six hours into his day by the time Eddie Leonard pulled his postal truck to a stop at the entrance of the Corwin's neighborhood and set off on foot to deliver the day's mail to the dozen up-scale homes leading up to the cul-de-sac.

Eddie had spent five days a week for the past four years delivering mail to the suburbs of Los Angeles, and as the unseasonably warm weather drew sweat on his brow that afternoon, he'd had just about enough of it.

Last street. You can do this, Eddie told himself as he made his way to the arc of the cul-de-sac.

The thought of skipping over the Corwin's house flashed in his mind for a few seconds as he gazed at the mailbox stuffed full of coupon mailers and magazines that obviously hadn't been collected in several days, but passing by the driveway, a package beside the mailbox caught his eye and he doubled back.

Eddie had no idea the importance of Bill Corwin's last—and only—communication with his estranged son and didn't give it a second thought until he made his way back to the truck. Lifting the roll-down door, he glanced at the address label for the first time, seeing if it should be sorted as local or out-of-town.

A local one.

Eddie tossed the package carelessly into the appropriate bin and latched the door behind him before making his way up to the cab of the truck and heading back to the post office.

In the rear of the truck, the day's outgoing mail rattled in white cardboard postal boxes. On the top of the heap was Bill Corwin's package. No need for a return address, his son's name was handwritten:

Jack Sanders.

About the Authors

Eric Enck is the author of four novels—including *Tell Me Your Name*—as well as dozens of short stories and non-fiction pieces. He lives in Delaware with his family.

Adam Huber is an editor and former journalist. *Snuff* is his first novel-length work of fiction. He lives in Philadelphia with his fiancé and two cats.

Both men consume large amounts of cheap whiskey and horror films.